DOUBLE TAP

DOUBLE TAP

THE SILENCER SERIES BOOK 6

MIKE RYAN

WWW.MIKERYANBOOKS.COM

1

Recker looked completely uncomfortable. There was no question he was out of his element. It was a day he knew was coming for weeks, and he wasn't looking forward to it at all. But he knew it was one of the give-and-takes that he had to do if he wanted Mia to remain part of his life. After three months of talking and deliberating, they finally decided on a place to live together. His apartment. His bare walls, his scant furniture, the barely livable arrangements, they were all about to go. Replaced by pictures, more comfortable surroundings, and things that smelled nice. And he wasn't all that warm and fuzzy about it.

"A little to the left," Mia said.

Recker closed his eyes and sighed, thinking if anyone saw him now, his reputation would take a severe hit. Well, maybe not severe, but he'd sure have to put up with a lot of ribbing and good-natured abuse. After all, hanging curtains wasn't exactly something anyone would ever expect to see him doing. He certainly never thought so.

But, it was the price he had to pay to be with the woman that he cared about. As long as nobody saw him do the homely duties.

"One day I'm shooting people and the next I'm hanging curtains," Recker mumbled to himself. "Unreal."

"What, honey?"

"Uh, nothing. Which way you want these?"

Though Jeremiah and his gang were now out of the picture, Recker didn't want Mia staying in her former apartment. He'd actually pleaded with her to quit her job and stay at home, that way he could be sure nobody would ever try taking advantage of her again. But that flew on deaf ears. Though Mia loved and wanted to be with him, she wasn't going to stash herself away and become a vegetable. She loved her job; she loved helping people, and she was determined to keep doing just that.

Recker still had concerns, but knew it was a lost cause in trying to change her mind. It just wouldn't happen. So he did the next best thing. He taught her how to be elusive. How to become invisible. And it wasn't just for her safety, but also for his. Nobody knew where he lived other than Jones. The last thing Recker needed was somebody following her and finding out where his home was. So they agreed that she would never drive straight home to the apartment after work. She would take a few extra turns to make sure there was nobody in her rearview mirror. Recker taught her which ways to go, and also how to spot if someone was tailing her. Over the previous month, he rigged up some practice situations where he used a different car to teach her how to, not only spot someone following her, but also how to escape them.

After a month of practice, Mia had gotten relatively good at the practice. She'd never be at a CIA level of elusiveness, but she wasn't half-bad. He figured if anyone ever attempted to follow her after that point, they'd most likely not be as good as he was. And if they were, they'd most likely find him eventually, anyway. She was at least good enough to satisfy Recker's worries for the time being. In any case, he'd continue working with her to sharpen her skills in the event she ever had to put them into use, which hopefully she wouldn't.

Once the curtains had been hung to Mia's satisfaction, Recker stared out the window for a few moments. As he was daydreaming, Mia continued unpacking some of her things, as well as some new things she'd bought for the apartment. Recker's gaze was interrupted as he noticed Mia putting some small, potted plants on the windowsill. He looked at her with a curious expression, almost like he wasn't sure what she was doing.

"What's that?" Recker said.

"Uh, plants."

"Why are you putting them there?"

"To decorate the apartment?" Mia replied, sensing that he was skeptical of her arrangements.

"Oh."

"Would you like me to take them down?"

"No. No. It's fine," Recker said, though he really did have some reservations about it.

"Are you sure?"

He tried to make a face to indicate he had no issues, though not very well. "Totally."

Mia smiled at him, thinking it was cute how he had

hang-ups over a few small plants. "It'll be OK," she said, patting his shoulder reassuringly.

"I'm fine. It's just I've never actually had plants before."

"Don't worry about them. I'll take care of them."

"Good. Cause I'm good at killing things. Plants probably included."

Mia laughed and gave him a pat on the shoulder as she went back to some of the boxes that were littered along the floor. He turned around just in time to see the horror of her taking out a few pictures that were already in frames. He stood there dumbfounded, his mouth slightly open, as he watched her nail the frames to the wall. There were some pictures of her, some of him, and some of them together.

"I need a case," Recker whispered. "I'm not made for this."

After putting a few pictures up, Mia turned around to grab another one when she noticed the blank expression on his face. Though she was amused at how uncomfortable the simplest of things seemed to make him, she tried to be understanding and not show it. She knew the barren landscape of the apartment before she got there was likely how his places had looked for the past ten years or so. It was probably all he ever knew. She walked over to him with a sad puppy dog kind of a smile and put her arms around him to give him a kiss, trying to be as sympathetic as possible. Though Mia was enjoying herself immensely, she knew it was hard for him. Change wasn't something that Recker was accustomed to or liked very much.

"It's going to be OK," she said. "I promise."

Her affection briefly helped to alleviate his anxiety over his changing life. A warm look into her eyes was enough to ease the fears of any man, Recker included. There was just something about the way she looked at him that made him feel more secure in his changing environment. At least when her arms were wrapped around him.

"When did you do all that?" Recker said, not aware that she ever had pictures of them made.

"Well, the pictures of us were the selfies I took of us. And the ones of just you were just pics that I took randomly. You've seen them before."

"I know. I just didn't realize that you printed them out."

"Is that a problem?" she said with a smile.

"No. It just makes things seem... permanent."

"I can take them down if it makes you uncomfortable."

"No, it's fine. I'm just... not used to looking at myself on the wall," Recker said.

Seeing the pictures of them together on the wall was a little jarring to him. In his mind, it was like a symbol of their relationship cementing. And though he still wasn't as comfortable with it as he tried to pretend he was, he knew Mia would be crushed if she had to take them down because of his uneasiness. It was just something he'd have to deal with.

Once Mia went back to hanging more pictures, Recker started feeling uneasy again. He started to think that maybe he just needed to get out of the apartment for a while. Maybe it was just the process of seeing all the changes unfold in front of his eyes that fueled his anxiety. Maybe if he went out and everything was done once he got back, he would feel much better about the situation. He thought maybe it wasn't the actual changes themselves that was causing his worries, and if everything was already done, it wouldn't bother him as much.

Recker pulled out his phone, praying that Jones had tried to call or text him. Even though he knew Jones hadn't, he hoped that somehow, he just missed the call. Maybe he didn't hear the ringer as Mia was talking to him about something. Or maybe he missed a text message when he was in a trance over what seemed like a strange apartment to him. But as Recker checked, his hopes were quickly dashed. There were no calls. No texts. But as he continued to watch Mia alter his apartment, or as he needed to get used to saying, their apartment, he knew he needed to escape for a while. Seeing he was supposed to have the day off, Mia was a little concerned when she noticed him looking at his phone.

"Everything OK?" Mia said.

"Oh. Uh, yeah. Yeah, everything's fine."

"Then why are you looking at your phone like that?"

"It's uh... it's David," Recker said, quickly thinking of something. "Yeah. He just texted me about something. I should probably call him back to see what's up."

"You were supposed to be with me all day," she said, disappointed about what she suspected was about to happen.

"Well, let me just see what he wants. Maybe it's not what you think."

Recker walked into the kitchen as he called Jones' number, hoping that the professor had somehow come up with a new case. The actual move-in day for Mia had already been postponed a couple of times when newer, more urgent types of cases had unexpectedly popped up at the last minute. Jones had personally assured her the previous day that nothing was on the horizon.

"David, I saw you called, what's up?"

"Um... what?" Jones said.

"So what's going on?"

"Nothing's going on. What call? I didn't call you."

"Oh. Well is it serious?"

"Serious? What are you talking about? Is everything all right there?"

"Yeah, everything's going fine here."

"I'm glad to hear it."

"So you really think you need me?" Recker said.

"Are we back to this again? What are you talking about?"

"Yeah, I suppose I can be down there in a while if you really think it's necessary."

"Michael, nothing is going on."

"She'll be disappointed, but she'll understand."

"Do we have a bad connection or something?" Jones said, looking at his phone in bewilderment.

"I can leave in about five minutes."

"Leave for what?"

"All right. I'll see you when I get there," Recker said, hanging up.

Jones sat there for a minute, trying to figure out what had just happened. He continued staring at his phone, lying on the desk. "I hope he hasn't gone crazy after less than one day of being domesticated."

Before going back into the living room, Recker looked at kitchen cabinets and let out a sigh. He wasn't that proud of himself for what he was about to do, deceiving Mia like he was. But he figured on the importance level as far as lies go, this one would rank on the bottom of the list. As he thought about it for a few more moments, he actually convinced himself it was better this way, anyway. Interior decorating wasn't his thing, and there wasn't much he could add. The only thing he could really do was get in the way. Mia would probably be better off, or at least faster, if she didn't have to stop every few minutes to massage his feelings over his changing apartment.

When Recker finally came back in, Mia didn't need him to say anything. She'd already overheard his conversation with Jones. Recker had made sure that he talked loud enough for her to hear. By the look on her face, he could tell that she wasn't pleased. She was just standing there looking at him, a picture frame in each hand, which were dropped down on each side of her by her knees. Recker started to open her mouth to explain before she stopped him. She lifted her left index finger off the frame and held it out in front of her, so he didn't say a word.

"I know," she sighed in frustration, yet still somehow mustering a smile. "You've gotta go."

"I'm sorry. It's just that something's come up."

"I know. I know. Something always comes up."

Recker walked over to her to try to smooth over her frustrations. He put his hands on her waist and brought her closer to him, giving her a gentle kiss on the lips.

"Bribery will not get you anywhere," Mia said, though the kiss wiped away the look of displeasure on her face.

"Are you sure?" Recker said, kissing her again.

"Well..."

"Besides, you'll get all this done a lot faster if I'm not here. You know I'm not really helping here."

"I just wanted this to be a special moment for us."

Recker knew it was important for her and took a moment to look around the room. "This isn't what's special. These things are just... things. The only special moment I need is when you're like this, when you're in my arms."

"You're lucky you're so good looking," Mia said, kissing him again, as all her displeasure faded away.

"I think it'll be better this way, anyway. You'll be able to do things the way you want without having to constantly look over at me to see if I'm hyperventilating."

"But what if I do something that you don't like?"

"I'm sure that everything you do will be perfect," Recker said. "Besides, the thing that matters to me most is that you're here. Everything else I can get used to. It might take some time, but I'll get used to it... eventually."

After a few more minutes of affection, Recker finally pulled himself away from Mia and went down to the office. And though she was initially disappointed at him leaving, she knew that everything would go by faster if he was gone. Not that her first priority was speed, but she didn't want to spend the whole day doing it either. When Recker got down to the office, about thirty minutes had elapsed since his phone call with Jones. Based on the strangeness of the conversation, the professor didn't know if Recker was actually coming or not. When he saw Recker enter the office, he stopped what he was doing and started peppering his partner with questions, wondering if he was losing his mind.

"Would you mind explaining what that phone call was about?" Jones said, getting up from his chair to greet his friend.

"Oh. I, uh, just needed to get away for awhile."

"Get away? Are you two already having compatibility problems on your first day of cohabitation?"

Recker thought for a moment. "What?"

Jones rolled his eyes, not believing that he didn't understand what he was talking about. "Are you two having issues already?"

"Oh. No. Nothing like that."

"Then why are you here? You both practically begged for a day off so you could fix up the apartment to suit both your tastes. And now you're saying you needed to get away?"

"Well, it's not a big deal," Recker said. "It's not like we're arguing or styles clashing or anything."

"Then what is it?"

"It's more or less me. I guess it's a little harder than I thought it'd be. Seeing everything transform from my way of doing things to a... more pleasant atmosphere will take some getting used to."

"Perhaps you're not as ready for this as you thought you were," Jones said.

"No, that's not it. I love her. I do. This is what I want. She's what I want. It's just... I've spent a lot of years doing things one way, my way. Not having to worry about what someone else would like or think."

"You'll adjust."

"I know. I just hope I don't drive her crazy in the process."

"Or me."

"So is there still nothing on the agenda?" Recker said.

"No. We're still clear."

Since he was there, and didn't have anywhere else to go, Recker sat down at the desk and went on the computer. He figured he'd just sit there for a couple hours doing busy work, trying to occupy some time before he went back home.

"So how long do you plan on continuing this little charade of yours and sitting here?" Jones said.

"I dunno. Two or three hours maybe. Why? Wanna get rid of me already?"

"No. Just wondering."

Jones also sat back down, though he had more definitive plans for his day. There were still a few cases that he was running down information on, but they were probably still a day or two away from acting on anything. His main goal for the day was finishing up on something that he'd been hiding from Recker. It was nothing like the last secret he was hiding from him, about Agent 17. This time, he assumed Recker would be pleased. At least he hoped so. After all, it was Recker's idea.

Finding another agent to work within their little group was something they'd discussed previously, and Recker knew Jones had started doing some work on it, Jones never divulged his progress or indicated how close he really was. Jones altered his search methods some-what this time, though. If there was anything that he learned from Recker's situation, it was that he didn't want to get another former agent who was in hot water. This time, Jones focused his efforts on finding ex-CIA agents who were no longer employed with the agency, but were still in good standing. That way they would never have to worry about being tracked or worry about being found. After an exhaustive search over the past several months, Jones finally targeted someone, firmly believing that he found his man.

Jones hadn't made any plans on when or how he'd tell Recker though. He figured it would be more of a feeling out process. Recker obviously wasn't good with change, and even though he initially seemed on board with the idea, Jones wasn't sure it'd be good to spring it on him now with the changes he had going on with Mia. But it was also something that he needed Recker's approval on. If they brought in someone new, it had to be someone they could both work with. Someone they had chemistry with. Especially Recker. If they were out in the field, Recker had to feel comfortable that a new person would have his back. That he could trust him. That was no small feat. When it came time to calling on the new recruit, Jones wanted Recker to be there to get his thoughts. Recker was good with initial encounters, and getting a feel on how people were.

Jones decided he'd wait a few more days before talking to Recker about it. He just felt that now wasn't the best time to make Recker's life even more chaotic. He'd give Recker some time to adjust to living with Mia and being in what was basically a brand-new apartment. It was going to be tough for Jones, though, not to spill the beans on what he thought was an exciting development. The man that he tabbed for the next member of their crusade was someone that Jones felt would be a great addition to the team. Someone that wasn't all that different from Recker. Well, hopefully for Jones there'd be one small difference... that he didn't have the same appetite for violence.

2

Jones waited another week before talking to Recker about the prospective new member of the team. He assumed that was long enough for Recker to get used to his surroundings. And if it wasn't, well, that was as long as Jones was giving him, anyway. With each day that passed, Recker seemed a little more comfortable with how things were going. He didn't seem as anxious or nervous about what was happening at home. Then, one morning when Recker came into the office, Jones figured it was time to clue him in on his activities.

"Everything going well in your new man cave?" Jones couldn't keep a playful smile from playing across his face.

"Don't get cute."

"I'm sorry. I just couldn't resist the temptation."

"Yeah, yeah."

"Drapes fastened, pictures hung?"

"You don't fasten drapes," Recker said.

"Oh. Well I see we are learning new skills, aren't we?"

Jones said, continuing the teasing. "Now you even know the correct procedures on curtains. My, my. If your enemies could only see you now."

Recker rolled his eyes, then looked up at the ceiling, contorting his face to make it seem like he was mad, though he really wasn't. "Are you done now?"

"Yes, I think so."

"Are you sure? Anymore quips or jokes? Might as well get them out now."

"No, I believe I'm done."

Recker sat down at the desk to start working as Jones walked over to him to spill the big news. Jones grabbed a file folder off the desk containing all his information before he approached his partner. He wanted to tell him early, before they got too knee-deep into anything.

"So, you remember what we talked about a few months ago?" Jones said, sitting on the edge of the desk. "About adding another person to the team?"

"Yeah." Recker wasn't paying Jones much attention as he typed away on the computer.

"Well, I've been thinking more about it."

"Oh? Finally come around on it?"

"Well, in a way. You're sure you're good with it?"

"Of course. It was my idea if you remember," Recker said, still not looking at him. "I mean, I don't want to add just anybody. As long as they got the skills and a personality that we'll both get along with, then yeah, I'm still good with it."

"Then perhaps you should look at this." Jones held out the folder.

Getting the clue that Jones had more on his mind

than he was saying, Recker finally stopped typing and looked at the professor. He glanced at the file folder, then took it out of his hands. Recker opened it, immediately seeing a picture and bio sheet of Christopher Haley. He intently looked it over for a few minutes before looking back up at Jones.

"This is the guy?" Recker said.

"Unless you have objections."

Recker turned his attention back to the contents of the folder. He read the bio sheet a couple of times before moving on to the other information that Jones had compiled on him. Jones had printed out everything he could find on Haley. Every case he worked on in the CIA, his life before he joined the government agency, and every detail since he'd left.

"Well, I'll let you read that without me looking over your shoulder." Jones walked around Recker and back to his own workstation.

Jones had probably compiled at least a hundred pages of information and notes on Haley. Not only the facts and details of Haley's life, but he had also added his own notes and thoughts. It was a meticulously prepared folder, something one would expect coming from him, bringing someone in to an operation such as the one they were running, one that would take Recker several hours to go over. Though Jones wasn't going to bug Recker about his thoughts until he was completely done consuming the file, he did keep an ear out, hoping to hear any sounds that Recker might make as he was reading. Maybe some grumbles if he didn't like something he read, or maybe something more lighthearted if he approved. Something that would give Jones an indication on which way Recker was leaning before they discussed it after he was done.

Unfortunately for Jones, Recker never gave any clues or hints on his thoughts as he was reading. He was stone-cold silent. And on something like this, Recker wasn't going to rush his way through. He was going to sit, read, and analyze. Possibly several times over. Jones knew he was going to be in for a long day. It occurred to him that maybe he should've given Recker the file toward the end of the day. That way he could've taken it home with him. Now, it was unlikely they were going to get any further work done. Luckily there was nothing pressing. After five hours of silence, without either man saying a word, or asking Recker a thing about his thoughts up to that point, Jones couldn't stand being left in the dark anymore. He needed some clarification about Recker's thoughts.

"So, what do you think?" Jones finally said.

"I'm still reading."

"I can see that. But surely you must have some thoughts at this point. Either one way or the other."

"Not yet."

"Come on, Mike. You've been reading for five hours. You don't have any inclination on which way you're leaning after five hours?"

"There's a lot to think about."

"Yes, I understand that. Does he at least seem promising?" Jones said, hoping to get even the littlest nugget of positive emotion out of Recker's mouth.

"Uh... maybe."

Jones sighed and scratched behind his ear, frustrated

that Recker wasn't going to humor him and tell him a thing. Recker wasn't going to do this on his own timeline.

"Do you think you'll have an answer today?" Jones said.

"Maybe."

"Oh, good lord. You're not going to give me the slightest of hints about anything, are you?"

"We'll see."

Jones knew it was a lost cause at that point. Recker wasn't going to tell him anything. And based upon the fact that Recker seemed to be reading the pages repeatedly, and he still had a few to go, Jones thought it possible that Recker might not even be ready to give an opinion before the day was over.

"Should I order a late-night snack?" Jones said, only partly kidding.

"Not something we should rush through."

"I'm aware of that."

"Maybe I should take this home with me tonight," Recker said. "That way I can have an answer for you in the morning."

"You're really going to put me through all that agony?"

"Why not? You're a patient person."

"In most cases. This doesn't happen to be one of those times."

"Why? What's so special about this? You seem very anxious for some reason."

"What's so special about this? We're talking about adding a number to our twosome. I've spent months working on this, finding candidates, discarding candidates, until I finally whittled it down to one. This one. So yes, I am a little anxious about this."

"Well I need time to analyze this. I can't give my thumbs up until I've fully vetted everything in here."

"Don't you think I've done that? Do you really believe I'd come to you with this unless I was absolutely sure on this?"

"What do you want? You want me to just rubber-stamp this?" Recker said.

"Of course not."

"Then let me dig into it on my own. I know you're anxious about it. Just relax."

Jones knew he wasn't going to speed up Recker's analysis, so he tried to block it out the best he could. He turned back toward his computer and started working again on some of the upcoming cases they had. He needed to do something engrossing, so he could forget about Recker reading the mountain of information next to him. The only thing he could think of was working on another case. And it worked. Jones completely blocked Recker out of his mind for the next hour until Recker finally made a noise.

"Crap," Recker said, drawing a concerned look from Jones, who thought he'd read something that he didn't like.

"What's the matter? What don't you like?"

"Nothing," Recker said, getting up from his chair.

"Then what are you doing?"

"It's past six o'clock. I'm supposed to be off today. Remember, I've got a girlfriend redecorating my apartment."

"Oh. I almost forgot about that."

"Yeah, well, I don't wanna be gone all day and night. She forgave me for coming. I don't know if she'll forgive me for staying indefinitely."

"What about Mr. Haley?" Jones said.

"I'll take his file with me and read it tonight."

"I was hoping I'd get a yay or nay from you tonight."

"Not likely. I'll have an answer in the morning," Recker said.

Though Jones wasn't especially pleased with waiting another day, he knew that was the best he was going to get. As Recker grabbed the file folder and walked toward the door, Jones tried one last time to get some information out of him.

"You're seriously going to just leave like that? You're not even going to give me a hint as to which way you're leaning?"

Without saying a word, Recker looked back and gave Jones a sinister smile, realizing he was torturing his partner without saying anything.

"You know, you have a mean streak in you," Jones said.

"Consider it payment for your needling about the curtains," Recker said, closing the door behind him.

In reality, Recker was very impressed with the file that Jones had accumulated on Haley. There were no obvious red flags that Recker could see. He spent eight years in the military, four of them in special forces, along with another eight years in the CIA doing clandestine operations. His assignments were for the most part carried out successfully, seemed to be highly thought of, and didn't seem to have any of the emotional baggage that Recker did. There really wasn't anything not to like. But Recker didn't like making decisions on the spot and wanted at least one night to stew it over. Plus, he knew that Jones wouldn't have recommended anyone unless he was certain it was the right pick. And there was a small piece inside him, enjoying making Jones squirm for the night as retaliation for teasing him the way he did.

When Recker got home, Mia had just finished the apartment. He walked in, hoping he wouldn't get the cold shoulder from her for being gone most of the day. As soon as he stepped inside, he was amazed at how different the place looked. It really did feel like he was in someone else's home. Pictures on the wall, flowers on the table, plants by the window, a couple extra lamps that he didn't recall having before. Mia really did do a wonderful job with it, he thought. And with everything finished, he hardly felt any anxiety over the latest changes.

He went over to the wall and stared at the pictures of them together. For the first time he could remember, at least since what happened in London, he finally felt at peace with himself. Looking at the two of them together, their cheeks pressed against each other, he felt like the emptiness he'd been carrying around for so long had gone away. He wasn't longing for Carrie anymore, wasn't wishing circumstances had been different, or that he'd acted in some other way. He was just relishing the fact he had found another woman who loved him unconditionally, much like Carrie did, and that he loved equally as well. For the longest time, he didn't think he'd ever find that feeling again. And for a while, he didn't think he even wanted it. But Mia changed all that.

As he was staring at the pictures on the wall, Mia snuck up behind him and wrapped her arms around his waist. Recker looked back at her and smiled. He turned around and kissed her, hoping she wasn't mad at him. By the warm smile she had planted on her face, he assumed that he wasn't going to get a tongue lashing, or the cold shoulder that he was worried about. As they stared into each other's eyes, Recker put his nose in the air, smelling something good coming from the kitchen.

"What smells so good?"

"Just figured I'd make a little celebration meal for our first night together in our new place," Mia said, her face beaming from ear to ear.

"Oh? What're we having?"

"Figured I'd go Italian tonight. Have some meatballs, spaghetti, lasagna, garlic bread."

"Wow. You're going all out. I don't know if I'll be able to eat all that."

"Smaller portions," she said gleefully, looking down at the folder that he was clutching in his hand. "What's that?"

Recker lifted it up as he explained what it was. "Just some work stuff."

"Oh. So how do you like the apartment?"

"It looks really nice," he said, looking around the room.

"Really? What bothers you about it?"

"Nothing."

"Really? There's nothing that's just eating away at you,

nothing that's making you wanna just rip it down and throw it out?" Mia said, sure that there must've been something he didn't like.

"No, really. Everything's fine."

"OK. It's just, I know before you left you were a little uneasy about everything."

"Yeah, I know, that was just me being... stupid. Honestly, everything's fine. I wouldn't change anything. Especially the woman who made it all happen."

Mia couldn't resist planting another kiss on his lips, happy that he seemed to enjoy what she'd done to the place. "Dinner's just about ready," she said, taking him by the hand and leading him into the kitchen.

Recker sat down at the kitchen table as Mia went to the stove and started bringing the food over. She already had plates and utensils set up, along with a nice table-cloth and a candle in the middle. Once she was done putting all the food down, she sat down across from Recker. She couldn't help but notice he looked a little out of it.

"What's the matter? Doesn't it look good?" she said, her eyebrows scrunched down.

Recker shook his head and looked up at her. "No, no, everything looks great. It's just uh..."

"What?"

"I don't think I've ever had a tablecloth on here. Or a candle," Recker said, trying hard to remember. "Come to think of it, I'm not sure if I've ever even eaten on plates here. Except the paper ones."

Mia laughed. "You know, that really doesn't surprise

me. You see these plates on the table? They're the only ones I found in the cabinets."

"Oh."

"I'm gonna have to go on a shopping trip. I've noticed you're a little sparse on a few things in here."

"That's the life of a bachelor."

"Well, that's over with now, right?"

"Looks that way," Recker said with a smile. "This might be your last chance to back out you know."

"Why would I want to do that?"

"Well, I'm not wanted by the CIA anymore, but it doesn't extend to the police department. Half of them anyway."

"I'm not really worried."

"You're not? If I'm caught, they could always arrest you as an accomplice or something," Recker said, warning her of the dangers, though it wasn't the first time they'd talked about it.

"And as I've told you before, you getting caught doesn't really worry me."

"It doesn't."

"No, you getting killed... that's what worries me. I mean, you're out there all alone most of the time, fighting against bad people," Mia said.

She was about to keep going but quickly thought better of it. The last thing she wanted to sound like was a worrywart of a girlfriend. Especially on a day like this, which was a big day for both of them. And she didn't want to be one of those girlfriends who was always nagging or crying about something. She knew Recker didn't need that either. She assumed that the quickest way her fears about Recker dying out would come true, were if his mind was filled with drama at home. Worrying about her instead of focusing on whatever his assignment was. Mia was determined not to do that to him. At least as much as possible. She knew there would eventually be fights or disagreements, as in any relationship, but she was going to try her hardest to not let it be over silly stuff or things that could be avoided. If the unthinkable ever happened, and Recker died out there on the streets, it wouldn't be because of her.

"Well, we're taking some steps to make sure that doesn't happen," Recker said.

"What do you mean?"

"David and I are talking about bringing in another guy. Another Silencer."

Mia laughed at the way he referenced himself. "You just love calling yourself that, don't you?"

Recker smirked. "Yeah, a little bit."

"So, you're really thinking about bringing another person in?"

"That's what the folder's for. David's narrowed it down to one person."

"Why didn't you tell me about this before?" Mia said.

"I didn't know. David just gave it to me today. I didn't realize he was this close."

"So, what do you think?"

"His package looks good," Recker said, admitting to Mia what he wouldn't to Jones.

"You think you'll be able to get along with another guy?"

"Yeah, if he isn't a pompous jerk," Recker said with a

laugh. "Besides, maybe that'll free me up at night for more time here with you."

"Well I'm definitely all for that."

"We'll see what happens. But having another person would definitely take some of the strain off."

"I'll be glad when or if it happens," Mia said. "I've always worried about you not having anyone out there watching your back. Especially with some of the situations you wind up getting yourself in."

"You mean the situations other people make me put myself in."

"So, when are you gonna make a decision on this guy?"

"I'll give David the go-ahead tomorrow morning when I go in. I just wanna reread everything to make sure it's the right call."

"Well you've always had great instincts on people. What's your gut say?"

"That he's the guy."

3

Just as Recker promised, when he came into the office the following morning, he was ready to give Jones his decision. The professor had a tough time sleeping and was awake before the sun came up. He was excited about possibly adding to the team, as well as anxious as he waited for Recker's answer. When Jones first started his search for a new member, he didn't anticipate he'd ever be that thrilled over it. He certainly wasn't that enraptured when the list of candidates first started appearing on his screen. He and Recker had developed a strong friendship and special chemistry. They couldn't do the work that they did without a powerful bond between them. He worried that a new person would possibly disrupt the dynamic that they'd built up. Jones' hopes weren't even that high at first. Finding someone like Recker, who would fit within their team, wouldn't be an easy task. He wasn't sure if it was even doable. It would be like catching lightning in a bottle twice, he thought. But as his search progressed, and he got further along and started diving into some of the candidates' backgrounds, Jones got a little more excited over the prospects of finding that elusive new member.

Jones had whittled the final list of candidates down to three before he selected Haley. In Jones' search parameters, he limited his search to men and women that were single. He assumed those that were married would have a more difficult time in making the move and doing the work that was required. Once the final three were chosen, it really didn't take Jones very long to narrow it down to Haley. As Jones made up the list of the desired attributes, Haley was the only one who checked off all the boxes. He was single, good with firearms, excellent at blending in, and willing to do the most difficult assignments. That was shown by his CIA case record. Haley had been stationed all over the world, Russia, China, North Korea, Africa, the Middle East, Europe, and South America, and spoke several languages. He'd been assigned at various points of his career to take out dictators, drug lords, firearm dealers, and corrupt politicians. His history was as promising as Recker's was when Jones first saw his file.

"You know, I miss the days when I used to beat you into the office," Recker said.

Jones was sitting at the computer typing away, but stopped at Recker's wisecrack. He turned to look at him. "By days, you mean one or two? Because I don't remember any more than that."

"Yeah, well, it's gonna be harder to do now you're living here. Now I won't even have a chance."

"Longing for nostalgia of our days of yesteryear already, are you?"

"What?"

"Nothing. Speaking of nostalgia and things that used to be and are no more, what is your opinion about Mr. Haley?" Jones said.

Recker tossed the folder down on the desk and sighed. Though he was still in favor of adding someone to the team, it was still a new wrinkle. It was another change that he'd have to get used to. Even though he wanted help, he still wondered how he'd react to another guy invading their space, especially when he had a bad enough time watching pictures get hung on the wall of his apartment. He wondered how he'd feel that first time he saw Haley do something that Recker was used to doing. Would he feel grateful, or thankful that he had help? Or would he feel jealous or threatened that someone else was doing his job for him? After a few more moments he came to his senses. He figured he probably wouldn't feel grateful or threatened. After all, there were plenty of bad guys to go around. Recker didn't have the market on them all to himself. There was more out there than he could deal with on his own. And that's what it was all about. Just getting the job done. By whatever means possible.

"I'm good with him." Recker said, finally admitting the truth.

"Hallelujah. I had ideas that you might not ever say what you really thought about him."

"I thought about it."

"I'm sure you did."

"Did you know all along, or did you just come to that conclusion overnight?" Jones said, wondering for his own amusement.

"I had a pretty good idea yesterday."

"Would it have killed you to at least say you were leaning in that direction, instead of making me wonder all day and night? And morning for that matter."

"It might have."

"Somehow I knew you would say that."

"So, what's your plan?" Recker said.

"With?"

"Haley. I mean, I assume you're not gonna just send him an email or a telegram and pitch him our little operation. Right?"

"Of course not. I was planning on seeing him in person and making him an offer."

"When will you be back?"

"When will we be back?"

"We? What do you need me for?"

"Because he's a highly dangerous man that I would like to have some backup on... just in case," Jones said.

"You recruited me alone."

"If you recall, there was some added muscle I hired at first to direct you from the airport. In case you weren't as cooperative as I'd hoped."

"Oh, yeah."

"So, are you ready?"

"For what?" Recker said.

"To go speak to Mr. Haley."

"Right now?"

"Do you have other plans?" Jones said.

"No."

"Well then there's no time like the present, is there?"

"A little notice would've been nice."

"Turnabout is fair play, is it not? You gave me no advanced notice on your thoughts last night. Therefore, I'm giving you none now." Jones flashed a devilish smile.

"You know, sometimes I think my personality may have rubbed off on you too much."

"I know, and it really gives me great pause for concern sometimes."

"How far is this excursion of ours gonna take us?" Recker said. "The one thing missing in his file was where he's at now."

"It's a short trip. He's in Baltimore."

"A nice, short drive."

"We'll be back before dinner. In time for you to hang more curtains tonight."

"Don't start that again. Besides, Mia's working the late shift."

They gathered up a few things from the office and began the drive down to Baltimore. It was only a two-hour drive so they would get there right around lunchtime. Haley was working for a home security systems company, so Jones knew they'd find him at his apartment. Thirty minutes into their drive, Recker had some questions about their upcoming encounter.

"What if he's got other things to do, and he's not there?" Recker said.

"Well then we'll wait until he gets there."

"Easy as that, huh?"

"Easy as that," Jones said.

"Nervous?"

"No. Why?"

"Just wondering. Isn't every day you try to recruit a new member for the squad."

"I've done it before."

"So, what's bothering you?"

"What makes you think something is bothering me?"

"Because I know you. You're not saying much, and you keep looking out the window like you're distracted by something. Unusual for you," Recker said.

"Just thinking about some things."

"You wanna spring it on me?"

"Just thinking about Haley."

"What about him? Having second thoughts already?"

"No. Just a few things I don't understand yet. There's a lot to be learned from his package. You can learn a man's history, his strengths, his weaknesses, but you can't learn everything. Some things you just can't tell until you meet someone and interact with them for a while," Jones said, still looking out the passenger side window.

"What are you getting at?"

"Haley left the CIA two years ago. And in that time, he's had four jobs. Worked in Virginia as a construction worker, in Pittsburgh at an industrial plant, in Delaware as a private security guard, now in Baltimore as a home security guard."

"Can't hold anything down," Recker said.

"I don't understand it. A man with his background, with his record, and he hasn't held onto any of those jobs for longer than six months. He's on his sixth month now with his current job. How do you figure it?"

"My guess? He's unsettled. He's looking for something. He's looking for a home, some sense of belonging. Something to hang his hat on. He's unsatisfied in his work, he's looking for more, and he hasn't found it yet."

"Well if that's true then that may work in our favor," Jones said. "That may make our offer more appealing."

"It probably happens to most guys who've done what we've done. You risk your life for your country and live in continuous danger and, then when it's all over, you find yourself schlepping around a broom somewhere. You feel like your work used to be important. You used to matter. Then you wind up a civilian and find out nobody gives two hoots about you anymore."

"It didn't happen to you."

"I guess I got lucky when I ran into you. Plus, I had something to keep me going. I didn't exactly go out on my own terms like most guys. It's probably also easier for those guys who have a wife or kids, some family to keep their spirits up. Haley doesn't seem to have that going for him."

"No, he doesn't. Never married. No kids. No immediate family to speak of. His father died when he was twelve, and his mother passed away three years ago to cancer. No siblings."

"Didn't he have a couple cousins or something?" Recker said, remembering the file. "Thought I read that in there somewhere."

"Yes, a few cousins down in North Carolina. As far as I can tell he hasn't spoken to them in some time. At least ten years that I could see. Has an aunt and uncle in

Denver. Hasn't had contact with them in at least the same amount of time."

"Classic loner."

"I hope not. If he's too much of a loner, he may not be willing to join us," Jones said.

The two of them continued talking about Haley for the rest of the drive. They talked about his background, what would make him so useful to the team, and some of the records that Jones unearthed of him in the CIA. He posed some hypothetical questions to Recker to see how he would have handled some of the situations that Haley found himself in on certain assignments. Most of which Recker said he would have done the same way. They continued talking about Haley the rest of the way to Baltimore, rolling into the city at 11:30 and finding his apartment without much trouble. He had a third-floor unit in a decent area. It wasn't upscale, but it wasn't the bottom of the heap either. Once Recker and Jones got off the elevator on the third floor, they walked to Haley's unit, looking at each other as they stood at the door, making sure neither wanted to turn back before continuing. It was their last chance. Neither did, though. Jones knocked on the door. Haley answered almost at once.

"Can I help you?" Haley said.

"I certainly hope so," Jones replied. "I guess there's really no easy way to get into this, so I'll just get right to the point. We're here to offer you employment."

"Subtle," Recker said.

"I've already got a job."

"Yes, I know. I mean we're here to offer you something

meaningful, something you can feel you belong to," Jones said.

"I'm not interested. Thanks."

Haley was about to close the door when Jones knew he had to think of something fast to keep the dialogue flowing. "I know you've been searching for something since you left the CIA," Jones said quickly. "We can help with that." He talked in his normal tone, and Haley stopped the door from closing.

"How do you know I worked for them?" Haley said, looking at the two visitors more closely, thinking that Recker looked like an agent.

"We know everything about you," Jones said. "If we can come in, I can explain everything in greater detail."

"But first, if you could put the gun away that you have hiding behind the door we'd appreciate it," Recker said finally, with a smile.

Jones looked at Recker, then back at Haley, feeling a little uneasy that a gun was being pointed at them if he was correct, which he assumed he was.

"We're not here to hurt you," Jones said, hoping to ease the man's fears.

"If we were we probably wouldn't be standing here asking to come in," Recker said.

Haley knew they were right. If it was somebody gunning for him, they wouldn't give him the courtesy of knocking on the door. They'd shoot first, then exchange pleasantries after he was dead, though it would be one-sided at that point. He tucked the gun inside the belt of his pants and opened the door for his two visitors to enter. Recker and Jones walked into the living room and sat on opposite ends of a couch. Haley sat on a sofa across from them, ready to listen to what they had to say.

"So, are you guys with the agency?" Haley said.

"I used to be," Recker said.

"We're both currently in the public sector. We have nothing to do with any government agencies." Jones watched Haley carefully as he spoke.

"So, what's this offer you were talking about?" Haley said.

"We're here to offer you a job. I assume you're not satisfied with how your life is currently tracking considering you've had four jobs in four different cities in the last two years."

"How do you know all this?"

"Information is something that comes easily to me. Doing something with that information, well, that's where you would come in."

Haley threw his hands up, not sure what his guest was saying to him. "What does all that mean exactly?"

"The short version is that we try to stop bad things happening to good people. We stop robberies, murders, assaults, kidnappings, all before the perpetrators have a chance to enact their crimes. Well, mostly anyway."

"How can you do that?"

"Like I said, information is something that comes easily."

"I don't understand what you need me for. If you get all this information, then why don't you just go to the police?"

"I suppose it's because, technically, my information is

gathered through illegal means. Software programs that I've enacted that I learned from my time in the NSA."

"You were in the NSA?"

"At one time. A long time ago. And I learned that there's a lot of good people, innocent people that could be helped by us, that otherwise would just fall through the cracks," Jones said. "Unless we did something about it."

Jones had brought a small computer bag with him and opened it, removing some folders and a couple binders. He put them down on the table in front of Haley for him to look through. It was examples of some of the work he and Recker had done in Philadelphia. News reports, press clippings, the cases they'd worked on, Jones figured that would be more helpful in helping Haley make up his mind than just talking of their exploits. When he first contacted Recker, all he had to go on was faith that their mission could be successful. And all he had was hope that Recker would go along with it. Now, he didn't have to do that. He had real-life examples to show. There were noted cases where it was documented how much of a help they were. But Jones also wasn't going to shy away from admitting the pitfalls either. He was going to be upfront and honest in telling Haley that, though they'd be doing important work, he wouldn't be on the same side as the law. At least in the eyes of the police department.

Haley eagerly looked through the information that was presented to him. He'd already heard of The Silencer, as some of Recker's exploits had become known throughout the east coast. But to sit and have him sitting across from him, looking through some of their files, was something of a thrill for Haley. After hearing of some of their stories through newspaper or TV reports, Haley had always had thoughts of doing something similar. But he didn't know where to start or how to set up an operation like that, so it never got past the idea stage. He didn't have a Jones to oversee anything.

Jones and Recker were giving Haley all the time and space that he needed to go through the things they had provided for him, not eager to rush him into anything. They looked at each other a couple of times, both of them were confident that their approach was working. By the look on Haley's face as he consumed what he was reading, at the very least, seemed intrigued. Eventually, Haley picked his head up to look at his guests, plenty of questions going through his mind.

"I have to admit that I've heard of you guys before," Haley said. "You've kind of made a name for yourself."

"Sometimes too much," Jones said, giving Recker a glance.

"I guess I still have sorta the same question. What do you want with me?"

"Well, our reasons are many. First of which, I'm not that handy with a gun, I'm not a whizz at tailing people, I'm not somebody who excels at close-quarter combat. That's what Mike does. He's the one who's mentioned in all these stories."

"But none of that happens without David," Recker said, making sure Jones got his due and equal share of the credit.

"What I'm good at, is finding the information that

these people need help. How I do that is a more complicated answer for another time. But what we're really looking for is another person out in the field, who can help in whatever situation is necessary. We've encountered several situations in the last year or so where another person would have been very useful."

"I'm good, but I can't be everywhere," Recker said.

"And you guys want me to join you?" Haley said, a little awestruck.

"That's why we're here," Jones said.

"I'm sure there are others who may have something better to offer than me."

"I analyzed thousands of files. I couldn't come up with anyone."

"My last couple of years haven't been filled with much to be proud of," Haley said.

"What you need is to be redirected," Jones said. "You need guidance, structure, something important to fight for. We can provide that."

"We can also provide the danger and getting shot at." Recker couldn't resist the quip.

Jones turned to look at his partner, giving him a disapproving look. "By the nature of our work, you will be placed in... difficult situations. That will be unavoidable."

"I'm not afraid to be in danger," Haley said quickly. "If you've seen my file, you know where I've been."

"We know. But I should also point out that even though you'll be doing the right thing, helping people, you will not be a friend to the police department. You will, at some point, become a wanted man. Unfortunately, there is no way around that. Your life as you know it will be over. You'll live and operate in secrecy."

"Living in secrecy's never been an issue for me. What about supplies, guns, stuff like that? Do I bring my own?"

"Whatever you wish. Bring whatever you like. Though I should warn you and point out that Mike has an extensive collection of weapons. Guns will be the least of your worries. Guns, money, vehicles, nothing will be an issue. Everything you will need will be at your disposal."

"Sounds good."

"There's only three things you will need to worry about," Jones said.

"What's that?"

"Successfully completing your assignment, staying out of public view as much as possible, and staying alive."

"Three things that aren't an issue for me."

"Now, we have had our fair share of publicity for whatever reasons, but we try to avoid being put in the spotlight. The more media coverage we get, the more police attention we receive as well. We obviously would rather not have either."

"Works for me. I couldn't care less about attention," Haley said, seemingly on board with the proposal.

"So far, this has been a two-man operation. We have no egos, no ulterior motives, nothing else matters except helping those who need it."

"I don't have an ego to check. I'm all about doing whatever's needed. I've always been a team player."

"That's one of the reasons we're here," Jones said. "Your file indicates you'd fit in."

"Would we work as a pair or separately?"

"Sometimes both. It all depends on the type of case and how many we're working. Everything's on the table."

As Jones continued talking about their operation, Haley kept looking through the files and documents that were laid out on the table. He was trying to soak in as much as possible. Though he tried not to show it too much outwardly, Haley was ready to burst out of his seat to accept the proposal. He had nothing there that was holding him back. And it seemed like the perfect opportunity to get back in the game. This was the type of work he enjoyed, and he knew he was good at. Since leaving the CIA, he'd been searching for something to fill the void. This would be the chance he was looking for to feel like his work mattered again.

"What made you leave the agency?" Recker said. "I didn't see anything mentioned in your file. You could've stayed on a few more years if you wanted."

"Yeah. There was a woman. A girlfriend," Haley said, looking depressed the moment he thought about her.

"Well, that's eerily familiar," Jones said.

"What happened?" Recker said.

"Mike, that's not our business."

"No, it's fine," Haley said. "I'd rather have everything out on the table with you guys. I'm not hiding anything. I met a girl, and I fell in love with her. Was with her for a few years. But she got tired of the frequent missions which meant I was out of the country all the time. So, I agreed to leave the agency to preserve our relationship."

"I guess things went sideways?" Recker said.

"Yeah, you could say that. I was out of the country for

about two months on my final assignment. When I came back, she was gone."

"She just left you?"

"Yeah. At first, I tried to look for her. Took a job down in Virginia to get by while I was searching. Then, after about six months, I found her. I used some contacts of mine from the CIA and found her living in Pittsburgh. So, I went there."

"And?" Jones said.

"She was with another man. She apparently met him even before I gave my notice," Haley said. "So, then I just kind of bounced around at a couple jobs till I wound up here."

"And you didn't kill either of them?" Recker said, half-jokingly.

Haley laughed. "No. Not that I didn't have thoughts about it. But, no, they're both living, safe and sound, happy as can be I guess."

"Pity."

They talked for another couple of hours, Jones continuing to give Haley the rundown about how their operation worked, what would be expected, and what, if anything, Haley needed. Once they were finished, Jones started picking the papers off the table, and put them back in his computer bag. He looked at the time and figured they needed to be getting back to Philadelphia. It was already past three.

"Well, we should be heading home," Jones said, reaching into his bag for a business card and handing it to Haley. "Take a few days to make your decision. Think about it. I'd appreciate a phone call when you've made up your mind. Either way."

Haley took it and looked at it briefly, before handing it back to Jones. "I don't need this. And I don't need a few days to think about it. I'm in," Haley said happily.

"Are you sure?"

"Definitely. I've got nothing keeping me here. This is the type of work I'm made to do. This is what I'm good at."

"Just to be clear, we're looking for someone for the long term. We're not interested in someone who's only going to stick around a few months or so before looking for something else."

"That's not a problem. I'll be in it for the long haul. You don't have to worry about me," Haley said, knowing they had fears over his recent work history. "These last couple years with those other jobs, I was just trying to fit in somewhere. This is what I need."

Jones looked at Recker, who nodded his head in approval.

"Well then, it looks like we have a deal," Jones said.

"Welcome aboard," Recker said, shaking Haley's hand.

"What do you need me to do first?"

"Take care of whatever you need to do here. Pack up, quit your job, take care of any bills or anything else you have," Jones said. "Make sure there's no outstanding issues that someone might track you down for."

"I can let my job know today. Won't take me long to pack. A day at the most. I can be up in Philly by tomorrow night."

"How's your car?"

"My car?"

"Yes, does it run OK?"

"Well, it's got about a hundred thousand miles on it, but I haven't really had many issues with it. Why?"

"Make sure you're still here tomorrow morning," Jones said. "You'll be getting a delivery."

4

True to his word, after getting back to Philadelphia, Jones placed an order for a brand-new car to be delivered to Haley's address. To be specific, a silver Ford Explorer. It was just about noon when Haley heard the knock on the door. It was a salesman from the auto group who was dropping the car off. Prior to that, Haley really wasn't sure what kind of delivery he was getting. Jones didn't say anything definite and didn't mention a new car specifically. Since his car was still running reasonably well, without any major issues, Haley definitely didn't envision the delivery being a car. And a new one at that. As soon as Haley finished signing for it, he reached into his pocket for the card that Jones gave him with his phone number on it and dialed.

"Mr. Jones, I really don't know what to say about this new car."

"First off, you can dispense with the Mr. Jones. David will do fine."

"I really want to thank you for this."

"Don't mention it," Jones said. "It's just what I like to consider a signing bonus."

"It's tough for me to accept something like this. I mean, it's a lot of money."

"Money will be the least of your worries. Once you're three months on the job, you'll have earned that new car at least ten times over."

"OK. Well, I already had my car packed with my things, so I'll transfer everything over to the new SUV and then I'll be on my way," Haley said.

"Excellent."

"So, I should be there in about two or three hours I would think. Where should I go exactly?"

"Great. Once you get near the Philadelphia exit, send me a message, and I'll text you the address."

As soon as they finished their conversation, Jones continued his computer work, almost ready to assign a new case. Recker was due in the office any minute. He had stayed at home for the morning since there was nothing for him to work on just yet. Though he hadn't shunned any of his work duties since being with Mia, Jones had to admit that he missed Recker hanging around the office more. Now when there were lulls, Recker usually chose to stay home with Mia when she was off from work. Before they became an item, Recker usually just did some busy work in the office. Jones missed the banter and camaraderie that he often shared with his friend. Though he still had that relationship with Recker, it just wasn't as much as before.

Recker came in after one, looking as calm and

refreshed as Jones had seen him in a long time. It'd been a few days between assignments, but it was something more than that. Jones assumed that his newfound home life was beginning to agree with him. For the last few days, Recker had no issues or anxieties over his changing apartment. After exchanging some brief pleasantries, Recker sat down at a computer next to Jones and started typing away. Jones turned toward his friend, unable to turn down what he thought was an easy target.

"You look very... relaxed," Jones said.

"Yeah, I guess I feel pretty good."

"I take it life at home with Mia is... soothing."

Sounding like Jones was hinting at something, Recker stopped typing and simply scrunched up his face as he looked at the screen, wondering what exactly his partner was trying to say. Recker started to say something but quickly thought better of it. If he was joking about his sex life, as Recker believed he was, he was just not going to get into it with him. Even in teasing, Recker was not comfortable in discussing that aspect of his life, no matter how close he and Jones were.

"Everything's good," Recker said, changing the tone of the conversation. "Apartment's set, curtains are hung, bedroom's squared away, it's all good. And I'm fine with all of it."

"I'm glad. I'm glad."

"Good," Recker said awkwardly, hoping Jones would talk about something other than his home life.

Like he was reading his mind, Jones did flip the discussion to other topics. "So, I just talked to Chris a little while ago. He's on his way."

"Great. When's he getting here?"

"Probably should be about an hour or two from now."

"Hopefully we can work him in slowly," Recker said. "Let him get a feel for the area before he gets thrown into the fire, let him get himself situated."

"Well, that's the hope. Unfortunately, we don't always get to pick the ideal scenario for things in our business."

"Speaking of which, what's up with that case you were telling me about? Ready yet?"

"Just about," Jones said. "I'm waiting on one more piece of information before letting you handle it."

"Which is?"

"A time."

"Already have the address and the perpetrators involved. Just need the date and time."

"What's the case?"

"Home invasion. Or it could just be a robbery. I'm still not sure about that."

"Oh good. Haven't had one of those lately," Recker said. "Who's the target?"

"Elderly couple in their seventies. Wealthy, no children in the house."

"Who are the suspects?"

Jones reached across the desk and shuffled a few papers around until he found the one he wanted. He looked it over briefly before sliding it over to Recker, who picked it up and analyzed it. He read the names and rap sheets of four individuals who appeared to be very violent in nature.

"How'd you get wind of this?" Recker said.

"Text messages between two of them. Seems one of

them works as a handyman on the side and was in the house last week on a job. If only people knew how vulnerable texting is. People assume that their conversations are private, like they're just handing a letter to someone in person."

"Yeah, well, it's better for us that they don't."

"In any case, he apparently found the home to be extremely desirable when he was there and let a few of his friends know the same."

"It's just the three?"

"How many do you want?"

"Four's fine."

"Anyway, they've all got criminal records, they've all been noted to use firearms, and they've all done jail time. A very rough crew."

"You said home invasion or robbery," Recker said, knowing there was a massive difference between the two options. "That's kind of..."

Knowing what he was about to say, Jones put his hand up and nodded, acknowledging the difference. "I know. They apparently can't make up their mind about how they want to handle the situation. One wants to go in forcefully, regardless of who's there or not, and the other one wants to wait until the homeowners are gone to rob the place. The third one doesn't really care in either instance and the fourth one says he's only interested in doing a robbery, and if it's a home invasion, then he's out."

Recker continued reading the information about the crew, shaking his head. "Great crew. That actually makes them a little more dangerous."

Jones raised his eyebrows, not sure if he agreed. "Definitely more unstable."

"The more unstable they are, the more dangerous they become. More unpredictable."

"You'd prefer a more professional crew? One that was in unison?"

"Actually, yes. At least then you can kind of guess what they're gonna do and how they'll act. With these guys, if they can't even agree on how they'll hit, you can't really assume how they'll behave once they're inside."

"Well they all have violent histories, so I'd say they're capable of just about anything," Jones said.

Recker and Jones continued talking about the case for a few more minutes, before one of the computers started beeping. It was one of Jones' software programs sounding an alert that something was developing. Jones quickly swiveled his chair over to that workstation and eagerly read the screen to gauge the situation.

"Oh dear," Jones said.

"What is it?"

"It appears it's happening now."

"What is?"

"Our home invasion-cum-robbery. Apparently the top three have agreed. They just sent the fourth guy a message saying 'We're doing it now. Are you in?'"

Recker jumped out of his seat and rushed over to his gun cabinet. "The other guy reply yet?"

"He just replied back that he's in."

"How much time we got?" Recker said, closing the door after removing a couple of weapons.

"I would say an hour, tops."

"How long will it take me to get there?"

"If you leave now, you should be there in about twenty-five minutes."

Recker hurried out of the office and hopped in his SUV to get to the northeast home. The house in question was in a nice neighborhood of single family two-story homes, brick lined driveways, lush front lawns, full basements, and expensive looking cars. It was a wealthy area that looked more like the suburbs than the city. When Recker reached the development, thirty minutes had passed. Seeing a car in the driveway, Recker parked down the street until he was sure what he was dealing with.

"David, you need to tell me what kind of car the Tresselmans have."

Jones immediately pulled the information up on the computer. "It's a Cadillac. Why? Do you see something else?"

"No. Not yet."

"How do you propose to handle this?"

"Well, I got two choices."

"I don't believe I like either of them," Jones said.

"I haven't even said what they are yet."

"If I know you as well as I think I do, you're going to suggest you wait inside for our suspects to arrive and head them off at the pass, so to speak."

"And the other?"

"Does it really matter? We both know what you will wind up doing."

Recker let out a sigh that Jones knew him so well and that he'd become that predictable. "I'm really gonna have to start changing my tactics."

"Then I'll have to learn your tricks all over again. Just out of curiosity, what was your second option?"

"To jump them outside before they get inside."

"Too public."

"I know."

Their discussion was interrupted by the sound of Jones' phone going off. He quickly looked at it, seeing it was Haley.

"Hold on, Chris," Jones said, before going back to Recker. "Mike, Chris is on the other line. I'll get back to you in a second."

"Take your time," Recker said, as if nothing was happening.

"Chris, sorry, we just have something going on right now."

"Oh. I just wanted to let you know I'm about half an hour outside of the city," Haley said.

"Great. I'll give you the address of the office."

"Do you need me to help out with anything? I'm ready to go."

"I'm not sure it'd be fair to send you out on something blind, without getting a chance to settle in first," Jones said.

"Well, if you need something, just tell me what you want done, and I'll give it a shot."

"Quite literally, most likely," Jones whispered, taking a few moments to think it over.

Jones put Haley on hold as he went back to Recker to get his opinion. His first inclination was to send Haley to help, but didn't want to send him into something he wasn't prepared for. He also had hoped for Haley to get a little easier assignment at first.

"It's up to you, David," Recker said. "According to his records, the guy can handle himself fairly well."

"I just worry about sending him in without knowledge of the particulars."

"There's only one particular here, helping me stay alive and nailing these bozos."

"Very well," Jones said after more reflection. "I'm sending him in. I hope he'll get there in time to help."

"You and me both."

Jones hung up with Recker and went back to Haley. "Chris, I'm sending you to Michael's location. As soon as we hang up, I'll text you the address."

"Great. What's the situation?"

"Mike's at the house of an elderly couple which is about to be the subject of a home invasion. Four dangerous, violent men should be there within the hour."

"How should I handle it?" Haley said.

"However you and Mike deem necessary. Just remember, on any mission, you have two tasks, both of which are equally important. Protect those who need it and get back here in one piece."

"Ten-four."

As soon as he hung up, Jones texted Haley the location where Recker was. Haley was driving along the interstate at a nice, steady pace since leaving Baltimore, but now he pushed down on the gas pedal a little harder. He wanted to leave a lasting impression on his first assignment. He wanted them to know right away that they made the right choice in selecting him. In the day since he was offered the position, Haley felt rejuvenated, invigorated with life again. The last two years had been a drain on him, from having his girlfriend leave him, to going from job to job every six months. Now, he felt like he had a purpose again and he was excited to be doing something like he'd been doing for the government for so long. Though it wasn't the same thing, it was close enough for him.

Recker wasn't going to sit in his car and wait any longer for the crew to show up. He needed to get the Tresselmans out of danger before any bullets started flying. He got out of his truck and walked up the stone pathway to the front door, knocking on it as he looked around for any signs of trouble coming. After knocking a few times, Mrs. Tresselman eventually answered the door.

"Can I help you?" the elderly woman said.

"Yes," Recker said, still looking over his shoulder. He then pulled out a police badge and showed it to her. "I'm Detective Scarborough. I'm not sure how to put this exactly, but you and your husband are in a lot of trouble right now."

"Oh dear, we haven't done anything wrong."

"No, no, it's nothing you did. Did you have work done on your house last week?"

"Yes, we did."

"We got word from a confidential informant that one of those men was a very dangerous criminal."

"Oh, no."

"Yes, and we've since found out that he's recruited three of his buddies to come back to your house to rob you."

The old woman had a stunned look on her face, seeming to be in disbelief at what she'd just been told.

"I'm sorry to scare you, ma'am, but we have to hurry," Recker said. "We understand that they're going to hit this place any minute."

"What are we supposed to do?"

"Is your husband at home?"

"He's watching TV right now."

"OK. I need you and your husband to go somewhere safe for the time being until this is over. Do you have somewhere you can go?"

"Maybe we can go to a neighbor's house," she said.

"Perfect. Let's go get your husband and I'll take you over there."

Recker was let in by Mrs. Tresselman and walked behind her as they made their way into the living room where her husband was watching TV. She started to explain the situation to her husband, but started to get emotional and couldn't finish getting the words out, so Recker explained everything to him.

"I thought there was something funny about those guys last week," Mr. Tresselman said. "A couple of them seemed to keep wandering off like they were looking the place over. Kept mentioning how nice some of the things we had were. I told you something didn't seem right about them."

"I know," Mrs. Tresselman said.

"I'm not sure how long this will last," Recker interjected. "Do either of you two need any medication or anything? Something you might need while you're gone."

"Oh, I have some heart pills," Mr. Tresselman said.

"I'll go get them," his wife said.

After taking a few minutes to get the medication they needed, Recker led the elderly couple through the home and to the front door. Before exiting, Recker looked out the window next to the door, pulling the end of the curtain back with his finger. He saw a car turning onto the street and coming toward the house. It was moving fast. Recker could only assume that they were about to be hit. Knowing it was too late to get the Tresselmans out of the house and to safety, he had to improvise his plan, like he so often did. He turned to the married couple in the hope that they may have their own solution to the problem.

"It's too late," Recker said. "Looks like they're on the way."

"What do we do?" Mrs. Tresselman said.

"You have someplace in here you can hide till this is over?"

"Maybe the basement."

"All right. You guys head there now as quick as you can. No matter what happens up here, no matter what you hear, do not come up under any circumstances. When it's over, I will come get you."

"We got it," Mr. Tresselman said.

"OK. Go."

Recker watched the Tresselmans scurry off to the basement, then turned his attention toward the window, watching as the incoming car approached. He went back into the living room, standing near the hallway which gave a clear view of the front entrance. As he readied himself, Jones called.

"I'm about to be real busy, David," Recker hurriedly said.

"Just hold them off as long as you can. Chris is on the way."

"No problem. I'll just toy with them for a little while."

Sarcasm aside, Recker had no illusions about holding the gang off. If they came in hot and heavy and rushed in quickly, he would have his hands full. His best bet was to pick one or two of them off as they came through the door. Less than a minute later, the car pulled aggressively into the driveway, the inhabitants quickly piling out. They burst through the front door without much effort, and as soon as the first two intruders showed themselves, Recker opened fire. The leader of the group, the man who set everything up, the worker who'd been at the home the previous week, was the first one through the door. He was also the first one to hit the ground after getting a bullet in the chest courtesy of Recker.

The second man through the door dropped to a knee and started firing his AR-15 assault rifle. Recker took cover behind the wall as bullets ripped pieces of the wood off, crumbling to the floor. Recker peeked around the corner with one eye, stuck his hand out and returned fire, though none of his shots hit the intended target. He took cover once again as more rounds from the assault rifle came whizzing by him. Knowing he was unlikely to win the battle against his opponent from where he was, Recker retreated to a more advantageous spot for him in the living room. The other two members of the crew came in through the front door, following in their partner's footsteps. Ducking behind a sectional sofa, Recker waited until he could hear the gang come into the room before he made his next move. He heard a heavy footstep walk across a creaky wooden plank that sounded like it came from beyond the edge of the hallway.

Recker rose up from behind the sofa and quickly located the intruders. He fired off several rounds in their direction before ducking for cover once again as all three members fired their assault rifles, making the couch he was hiding behind look like Swiss cheese. Recker crawled along the floor to the edge of the couch and fired a few rounds from the side, hitting one of the men in the leg. As they returned fire, a bullet hit his weapon, knocking it away from his hand, flinging it across the room. He reached around his back and removed his backup weapon, trying to think of his next move.

"This is not how I hoped this was going to go," he said to himself.

Knowing he was both outnumbered and outgunned, Recker figured his best move might be to reason with his opponents. If he could talk some sense into them, he might just live to see another day. He couldn't stand there and have a shootout with them.

"Police will be here any minute," Recker shouted. "Get out of here now while you still have the chance."

The new leader of the group replied almost instantly. "You killed our friend. We're not going anywhere until you get what you deserve."

"Revenge ain't so sweet if you're locked up because of it."

The gang didn't bother to reply and simply lit up the couch again, Recker hugging the floor as much as humanly possible, hoping the bullets would fly over the top of him. Luckily for him, his backup was just about there. Though he used the GPS on his phone, Haley still had a tough time finding the place. With not being familiar with the area yet, there were a couple streets that came up on him a little faster than he anticipated. As he pulled onto the street, with his window open, he could now hear the distinct sounds of gunfire. Haley gunned his brand-new SUV toward the house in question, squealing his tires as the rubber burned along the pavement. He hopped out of his truck and withdrew his gun as he ran toward the opened front door. He quickly surveyed the situation, seeing a dead body lying just inside the door.

Though he couldn't see anybody yet, Haley could easily define there were at least three people around the corner. He could make out the sound of a Glock handgun along with at least two assault rifles. From experience, he guessed they were AR-15's, and the shots rang out too close together to only be fired from one weapon. Haley slid down the hallway slowly, careful so as not to give away the surprise of his presence. He held his gun in front of him and pointed it toward the ground as he inched closer to the combatants, gripping the handle of it with both hands. As he got to the end of the wall, he peered around the corner, easily making out two men with assault rifles who were standing near a couch and pelting the room with bullets. With a point-blank shot, and his presence undetected, Haley knew he could pick off one with no problem. He just had to hope he could also get the second one before the guy turned himself and fired. Haley pointed his gun at his first target, aiming for the side of his temple. He gently eased his finger on the trigger. His target dropped immediately from the impact of the bullet.

Haley didn't bother to wait to see the final impact. He knew he got him as soon as he pulled the trigger. Immediately after squeezing the trigger, he took aim at his second target. It was easier than Haley was anticipating. His second victim noticed his partner drop to the left of him and looked down at his lifeless body before realizing that a second shooter had snuck in behind them. Haley fired three shots at the man's chest, knocking him to the ground before he even realized what was happening. Though he didn't perish immediately, death overtook him only a few minutes later.

The room fell deathly silent as Haley waited to see if there was another shooter. He poked his head around the corner, and almost got his head blown off, as the remaining member of the gang clung to the wall and fired when he saw the strange head appear past the corner. Haley quickly emerged and fired off a couple of rounds before ducking for cover again. The last gang member took a step away from the wall to get a better angle on the new shooter, giving Recker the chance he needed to get back into the fight. Recker jumped up from behind the couch and saw the intruder with his back turned to him, giving him a perfect shot. And he took it.

Recker fired four rounds in quick succession, though the first two bullets were all that was needed to get the job done. The man fell forward with a massive thud as his head slammed into the laminate floor. Recker looked around, waiting for whoever else was in the house. He hoped it was Haley, though he couldn't be sure that it wasn't the police.

"Recker?" Haley shouted. "It's Haley."

"It's clear," Recker said calmly.

Once Haley showed himself, Recker put his gun away, then walked over to where his first weapon landed and picked it up. As he holstered his weapons, Haley checked on the pulses of the four men they'd just shot. All were dead.

"Figured you could use some help," Haley said, taking his first opportunity to joke with his new partner.

"Ahh, you know, I had it under control."

Haley nodded and looked at the dead bodies on the floor. "I can see that."

"Took you long enough," Recker said, firing back with a tease of his own. "I mean, I wanted to see what you could do, so I was toying with these guys for a while. I was doing my best to hold back as long as possible for you."

"Oh, is that what it was?" Haley asked with a smile.

"Well, I wanted you to make a good impression for David."

The two men shared a quick laugh before Recker came over to his new partner and shook his hand.

"Thanks for the assist," Recker said, returning to a serious mood.

"I'm glad I could help. What now?"

"Now we hurry up and get out of here before the police show up. The homeowners are in the basement.

I'll let them know it's safe to come up and we'll be on our way."

"I'll wait outside for you."

Recker quickly scurried down the steps to the basement and let the Tresselmans know that everything had been taken care of. Trying to explain to them as quickly as possible to avoid any police entanglements, he told them who he really was. He didn't want to just leave four dead bodies in their house and just hope the police eventually arrived without giving them the satisfaction of knowing the truth about what happened. After they thanked him, Recker hurried out of the house before they had any more company that they'd have to deal with. Haley was sitting in his truck as Recker walked over to the driver side window.

"Everything's wrapped up here," Recker said. "We'll head back to the office and put a stamp on this. Ready?"

"Lead the way."

Recker got in his own car, leading Haley to the office. As they were driving, Haley felt pretty good about his first piece of action at his new job. It'd been a long time since he was involved in that type of altercation, but it felt good. Not the actual shooting or killing people, but feeling that what he did mattered, that it was important. He wasn't the only one thinking about what had just gone down. Recker was also thinking about Haley's first taste of action with them. For him, it couldn't have gone down any better. There was no doubt in his mind that Haley saved his bacon. It was a tough spot for Haley to be thrown into. He had no preparation, no heads-up, just tossed right into the thick of things. Sometimes it was better like that, Recker thought. But in any case, Haley proved right out of the gate he could be counted on as a pivotal member of the team. It'd still take some time to get used to each other, but Haley proved he could shoot, he wasn't afraid of close-quarter combat, and that he wasn't one who panics. Much like Recker, he dove right in and figured out the rest later. It was a good start to their relationship.

5

Recker had already called Jones on the way back to the office to let him know how everything went at the Tresselman home. Though Jones pressed for details, Recker didn't offer many. Jones was very curious about how Haley handled things on his first day, but Recker just told him that he was fine. No other remarks. Just fine. So, once the new Silencers returned, Jones was ready to pepper them with questions, excited to hear how things turned out.

"Mr. Haley, how did everything go?"

Haley took a quick look at Recker before answering. "It went good. Yeah, just showed up and did what I had to do," he said in an unassuming manner.

"I hated to drop you into a situation cold like that, right off the bat without a chance to get your bearings straight."

"Hey, it's the job. It's the way it was at the agency. I'm fine with it. Sometimes it's gonna happen like that. I'm just glad I got there in time."

"Mike?" Jones said, hoping to get his longtime friend's perspective.

Recker looked at Haley and nodded, giving him his seal of approval. "I can honestly say that things might have turned out differently if he wasn't there. He passes muster."

"What do you want me to do now? Another assignment?" Haley said, looking to Jones.

Jones smiled, appreciating his new hire's eagerness. "While I admire your zealousness, let's take a step back to breathe for a few minutes. Not to mention there's no other cases right now."

"Probably should start shopping around for an apartment," Recker said. "I can take you to a few spots if you want."

"No need, Michael. I've already taken the liberty of securing an apartment for Chris at Regal Apartments."

"Nice place."

Jones grabbed the brochure for the apartments off the desk and handed it to Haley. "I signed a six- month lease, but you're under no obligation to stay if you don't like it."

"I'm sure it'll be fine. I'm not picky," Haley said.

"Well, I just didn't want you to wander around aimlessly for a few days until you figured things out. I thought it'd be helpful if you at least had your lodgings figured out ahead of time. But like I said, if you don't like it after a few weeks, you're free to find something else."

"It really is a nice place," Recker said.

"I don't doubt it," Haley said. "If you've seen my last few apartments, you'll know I'm not very picky about where I live. As long as I don't need to booby trap the front door while I'm sleeping I'll be alright."

"I'm monitoring a few other situations as we speak, and though you never know when something will just pop up, it looks like it will be another day or two before the next case," Jones said, handing Haley the keys to his new home. "So, rest up, order some furniture, get yourself situated. Come back tomorrow morning and we'll start going over our operation in greater detail."

"Great. I'm ready to dive in."

Before he left, Recker stopped him with a few pertinent questions of his own. Well, he really only had one. "Chris, how much armor you got with you?"

"Armor?"

Recker walked over to his gun cabinet and opened it, letting Haley look over his arsenal. Haley studied its contents and picked up several of the weapons and accessories that were inside of it, looking thoroughly impressed by the collection.

"Wow, this is something," Haley said.

"You need me to make room?" Recker said.

"Nah. I only got two guns," Haley said, patting the handle of the gun inside his belt.

"Hmm. Not everybody shares your enthusiasm for firearms," Jones said with a snicker.

Recker gave Jones a disapproving glance, then looked at Haley, almost in disbelief that he didn't carry more weapons with him. Maybe Jones was right, maybe he did have an excessive love of things that caused massive amounts of destruction.

"Well, if you ever need anything, take whatever gets the job done," Recker said.

"Thanks."

"And if you wanna add to the collection, feel free."

Haley took a few more minutes to examine what Recker had collected up to that point, impressed with the amount and variety that he had stored. Though he was intrigued, and proficient in his own right, he didn't have the same love of weapons that Recker had. He knew how to use them, knew a lot about them, but they were just a means to an end for him. He didn't put much thought into it other than whatever he needed at the time. After Haley finished examining the gun collection, he bid his new friends adieu. Recker went over to a computer and started helping Jones decipher some information on a few upcoming assignments. Before they got too deep into anything, though, Jones had some more questions about the Tresselmans. He worried about Haley being discovered already.

"I've already started monitoring police and media communications," Jones said. "How much attention will this get?"

"Well, you've got a home invasion in a wealthy neighborhood, with two elderly citizens, which were stopped by me, and you've got four dead bodies to go along with it. What do you think?"

"I was hoping Chris' involvement in our operation would not get out for a while. Element of surprise and all that."

Recker shook his head. "Should still be good with

that. There were no witnesses, the Tresselmans never saw him. I already sent him outside when I talked to them."

"How about neighbors or people just happening to be walking by? Anything like that?"

"No, not that I saw. Should go down as just me being there."

Jones made a slight noise with his mouth as he thought of something. "That reminds me, I should talk to him about the notoriety he's likely to start receiving."

"What about it?" Recker said, not seeing what the concern was.

"Well, we both know that some people who start to read and believe their own press clippings... sometimes it goes to their head."

"I don't think that's something we have to worry about."

"I hope you're right."

"Nah, it won't be an issue. I think that's only a problem when you get someone who likes their work too much. He doesn't strike me as the type who gets caught up in the hype. I think he's pretty much like me. He's good at what he does, but he doesn't really get any pleasure or enjoyment out of it. Just do what you gotta do and move on. He'll be fine."

"Once again, you're probably right."

"Besides, how's anyone gonna know there's two of us?"

"You know as well as I do information spreads quickly. Take today, homeowner sees another man with you helping, sees you leave together, interacting with you, then tells police or the press there seemed to be another person with you. Boom, just like that, everyone knows there's two of you."

"Well you don't have to worry about that today."

"Good to know."

"You know it's going to happen eventually, though. And it'll probably happen sooner rather than later."

"I'm well aware it will happen eventually," Jones said.

"So why worry about it? It'll happen when it happens."

"Just because we know it will come to fruition at some point doesn't mean we shouldn't try to take advantage of the fact that we now have an extra person in play."

After a few more hours of work, Recker decided to kick back for the night. Mia worked until seven and Recker wanted to try to make it home around the same time she did. Part of him felt badly, though, as he knew he wasn't spending nearly as much time in the office as he used to. Not that he was shirking his duties at all, and whenever there was an assignment, he immediately responded whether he was at the office or at home. But after the last few years of him and Jones working hand in hand, often late into the night and at the expense of sleep, it seemed a little weird that he left a few hours sooner than he used to.

"Hey, you don't mind if I get out of here, do you?" Recker said.

"Not at all, why?"

"Just making sure you're good with it."

"Why wouldn't I be?" Jones said, not yet looking at him as he continued typing away at his computer.

"Well, it's sort of a new dynamic around here. Got a

new guy coming in, I'm not here as much as I used to be, I have the stuff going on with Mia, you know."

Jones smirked and turned his head to look at his friend, hoping to ease his fears. "I started preparing myself for these days when I first realized that you and Mia were heading in this direction."

"So, you don't have a problem with it."

"Of course not. These last few months are the happiest I've seen you since I've known you. It's been a refreshing change."

"OK. I just wanted to make sure."

"Besides, you haven't missed anything. You've been as reliable as you've ever been."

Recker then thought of something that hadn't occurred to him until now. "That's not one of the reasons you decided to get Chris, is it? As an eventual replacement for me in case I started drifting away because of Mia."

"Don't be ridiculous," Jones said. "If the thought ever entered my mind, it was only for a fleeting second. The basis for getting Chris was exactly as we've talked about. Getting you the help you could use, and sometimes need, as well as having the chance to help more people."

"Good. Cause whatever happens with Mia, I'll still be the person that you need me to be. That won't change."

"I know that. Regardless, we both know the office is more my domain, anyway. As long as you're out there where you need to be, that's what matters most."

Once their discussion was finished, Recker left the office and headed home. Mia had already sent him a text message that she was on the way. When Recker got to their apartment, Mia had beaten him there.

"I was hoping to beat you here," Recker said.

Mia smiled, just happy to see him. She greeted him with a passionate kiss as soon as he stepped foot through the door. "I missed you."

Recker smiled back at her once their lips disengaged and put his hand on her cheek, gently rubbing her cheek. She put her hand on his, soaking in the moment. She then kissed his hand and took it in hers, leaning in for another kiss.

"I could do this all night," she said.

"Not a bad idea."

"I guess we should eat first, though."

"If you really want to."

"I stopped on the way for sandwiches," Mia said, somehow pushing herself away from him.

She grabbed his hands and put them on her waist as she led him into the kitchen. They sat down next to each other at the table as they started eating. Recker had told her in the morning about Haley coming, and she was wondering how it went. She was hopeful that with another guy there, Recker's time with the operation might soon be coming to an end. Or at the very least, drastically cut back. Though Mia had made several suggestive hints over the past several months they'd been together, most of them she disguised as part of a joke, or her comment was so brief that she quickly moved on to another topic. But much like how she didn't want him worrying about her when he was working, she didn't want to nag about him doing something else either.

Though she'd be ecstatic if he eventually decided to live a quieter, more normal life with her, she wasn't going to beg or prod him to do it, or make him feel guilty about it. But upon hearing about the new guy in the fold, she couldn't help but think now would be the time to talk to him about her feelings. At least so they'd both know where each other stood.

"So, how'd things go today with the new guy?" Mia said.

"Good. I think it'll really work out well with him."

"How can you be so sure already?"

Recker finished chewing the piece of food in his mouth, then raised his eyebrows as he debated how much information he should divulge to her. If he told her the truth and said how much trouble he found himself in, he didn't want her to worry about it. Likewise, he also didn't want to blindly dismiss it, pretend it didn't happen, and lie to her. It didn't take him long to deliberate. He spent a long time being miserable after what happened to Carrie, and now he'd finally found himself happy again with Mia, he didn't want to jeopardize what they had by lying about anything. He figured there may be times when he had to shield her from the truth, whether it was for her own good or for whatever reason, but now wasn't one of those times.

"He really got me out of a tough spot today."

"What happened?" Mia said, putting her sandwich down to focus on him.

Recker explained the situation in detail, not leaving a single thing out. As he described everything, he could see the level of concern on her face as it contorted in different directions. After he finished, he waited for Mia to blurt something out that would indicate how troubled she was with everything. She didn't though. She tried to stay as calm as possible. She wasn't going to fly off the handle, or make a mountain out of a molehill, even though she was unsettled at the day's events.

"Well, it's good he showed up," Mia said, trying hard not to get emotional, though Recker could tell she was holding back.

"Yeah, seems like he'll be a good fit."

Mia wondered how far she should get into his profession with him, and calmly started asking some questions that she was thinking about earlier. "So... with a new partner, he should be able to take some of the strain off you, right?"

"In theory."

"That should mean you're able to take more time off, right?"

"That's the plan. To a point, anyway," Recker said, getting the feeling that she was working up to something bigger.

"Do you think there will ever come a time when you're no longer needed? Or maybe you won't want to do it anymore?"

There was the question that Recker was waiting for. He looked at her sympathetically for a moment, before letting his eyes fall to the table as he contemplated his answer. He didn't want to berate her for it, or dismiss her out of hand entirely. He knew she was trying not to sound like an overbearing girlfriend or try to influence his behavior. She wasn't trying to dominate him or make him submissive to her wants and desires. Recker wanted to answer tactfully and respective of her feelings.

"I don't know if there'll ever be a time when I'm not needed. I kind of doubt it. There's enough that needs to be done out there that we could hire five more people and it still probably wouldn't be enough."

"What about maybe walking away from it one day?" Mia said, finding it hard to look at him as she asked the question.

Recker's face looked strained as he tried to answer as delicately as possible. "I don't know what the future holds, Mia. Could there be a day somewhere down the line where I've had enough of this? I mean, maybe. I can't see that happening anytime soon, though. I like what I do, I'm good at it, and there's people out there who need me. People who could've gotten seriously hurt or killed if I wasn't around, including you."

"I know," she said, starting to backtrack so he didn't think she was trying to talk him into anything. "I'm not saying I think you should quit or anything. I was just wondering if you ever thought about it."

"I know. If that time ever did come, though, what would I do? I mean, this is basically, in one form or another, the only thing I've ever known in my adult life. I'm not really qualified to do anything else."

"Mike, you can do just about anything you want."

"Really? Because of that college degree I have? Or my design skills? Or because I have such talent in computer programming? Or... should I keep going?"

Mia sighed, understanding his point. "I know what you're saying. I'm just saying that I would hope at some point, even if it's the far distant future, that you would consider doing something else. Something less dangerous perhaps? Something where I wouldn't have to worry about whether you're coming home in one piece?"

Recker shrugged, not knowing what else he could tell her at that point.

"You could start your own business. Or just live a quiet life at home... with me of course," she said with a playful smile.

"That might not be so bad."

"You have enough money that you wouldn't have to do anything. You wouldn't have to reach for something."

"You know money is not something that motivates me."

"I know. I'm just saying that even if you eventually stopped doing this, you would never have to worry about a paycheck. You'd never have to worry about living week to week, or wondering how you're gonna pay for bills or repairs. You could wait until you found something else that you love."

"I already found something else that I love," Recker said.

Mia tilted her head and smiled, her heart almost melting, knowing that he was referencing her. The thought occurred to her though, that maybe he was saying it to get her to change the subject. If that was the case, she wasn't biting.

"Maybe start your own private security business," Mia said excitedly.

"Basically, the same thing I'm doing now."

"Except maybe not on the opposite side of the law."

"Technicality," Recker said, trying to lighten the mood.

Mia looked down at the table again, a somber look on her face. "I'm sorry," she said, thinking that she'd peppered him with too many questions.

"For what?"

"You probably think I'm nagging at you to quit or something."

Recker shook his head. "I don't think that."

"I told myself since that first night that we got together, that I wouldn't be one of those girlfriends that tried to change you or change who you are. And I won't."

"I know that."

"But sometimes it isn't easy knowing you're out there with guns pointed at you with men behind them that I know would like to kill you."

"That's why I try to avoid talking to you about things. It's probably easier for me to go through it than it is for you to wonder about how things are going," Recker said.

"I just hope I'm not going to be a sixty-year-old and still worrying about you doing the same thing out there," she said with a laugh.

Recker almost made a comment that he would regret, quickly stopping himself before the words left his mouth. He was about to tell her that he'd probably be long dead before sixty if he was still doing his current work, but realized that it would be an unthoughtful and unfunny comment. Luckily, he could see the foolishness of his words before he said them. He then thought of an alternative. Something that would probably be more soothing to her ears.

"I just hope if I make it to sixty that you're still with me," he said.

Mia shook her head. "It took me, us, several years to get to this point. I'm not gonna give it up now. If this is all you'll ever be, I'll be with you every step of the way. I'll never let you go. No matter what. I just hope you'll always feel the same."

Recker gave her a grin, then reached under the table to hold her hand. "I don't know how I'll feel in five or ten years. Maybe I'll still be doing what I do now. Maybe I'll still enjoy it. Maybe I won't, and I'll be ready to move on and try something else. I don't know. What I do know is that my life is better because you're in it. You make me a stronger person and a better person. Whether I'm here, or I'm in Boston, or Seattle, or Texas, or even Japan, wherever I am, I can only hope that you'll be with me."

Mia looked at him endearingly and gave that sexy smile of hers that he loved so much. "You're never getting rid of me." She leaned over to him and sensually kissed him as they both got into the moment. After a few minutes of kissing, their appetites turned to each other, leaving their half-eaten sandwiches behind as Recker scooped her up in his arms and carried her into the bedroom.

6

It'd been two days since the battle at the Tresselman home. A couple new cases appeared on the radar, and Jones split his new team up, much to Recker's displeasure. He wanted Haley to shadow him two or three times until he got the hang of things on his own. Jones, though, thought that would be a waste of time and manpower, not to mention unnecessary. Haley already proved on his first day that he could handle whatever was thrown his way. Jones didn't see the need to pair him up with Recker, unless the assignment called for it. But Jones also had another reason for keeping them apart at first. He wanted Haley to develop his own identity without any interference from Recker.

Recker was obviously a top-notch operator, and Jones couldn't ask for anyone better, but he didn't want Haley to be a carbon copy of him. He wanted Haley to have his own personality and his own way of doing things. Part of it was that he didn't want Recker molding Haley into that shoot first mentality that his partner sometimes had.

Jones hoped that Haley would, when the situation called for it, find a more peaceful solution than Recker usually looked for.

Though Recker thought it would be better for Haley to follow him, it wasn't something he was going to quarrel over. Jones didn't think that was the best choice and Recker went along with it without much of an argument. Also, as Jones pointed out, Recker didn't have someone showing him the ropes when he first started. It was just a trial by fire. And he handled it just fine. Outside of a few extra dead bodies than Jones would have hoped for. He assumed that Haley would also handle things just fine. While Jones initially thought that it might take Haley some extra time to get back into the swing of things after basically sitting out the last two years on the sidelines, his work at the Tresselman home seemed to indicate it wouldn't take as long as he anticipated.

While Jones was pretty comfortable with Haley handling anything coming his way, he still gave him the lesser of the two cases they were working on. Recker was assigned a murder for hire case, while Haley was given another attempted robbery. Unlike the first one that Haley handled, this one shouldn't have been as interesting. For one thing, there was only one suspect. The second, the person in question did not have the same violent tendencies as the previous gang did. Whereas the first group that Haley encountered all had extensive histories with firearms, the new case involved someone who did not have that same love of guns.

Recker's case was a little more involved as an out-of-state gunman was hired and brought in by a husband to take care of his wife. The man was a very prominent businessman whose wife was close to filing for divorce. Rather than go through that, and have a very large alimony payment, the man decided that killing her was the better option. Through some less than scrupulous contacts that the man had with a local crime syndicate, the plan was put into action. At first, Recker tried to find the shooter. That proved to be more difficult than first imagined and they had to change tactics, instead, focusing on the wife. Recker's job was tailing her wherever she went. The information that Jones dug up indicated the hit was supposed to go down today, but they just didn't know the exact time, or where it was supposed to happen. So Recker waited, and waited, and waited some more.

He'd been tailing the woman since 7am, and he followed her to a salon, several clothes stores, two shoe stores, a restaurant, an antique store, and finally a gas station. He saw no abnormal signs that anything was about to happen. He didn't question the intel that they'd received, but these were the cases that he hated most. Following people around aimlessly. Especially when they spent the bulk of the day shopping. It wasn't as much the waiting as what he had to do while he was waiting. He would've preferred to just sit in his car. At least that way he'd have the radio. Tailing people as they shopped for clothes and shoes was almost nauseating. He couldn't even pretend to be interested in that. He probably wouldn't have minded so much if they went to a gun store or something, but fashion just wasn't his thing.

Recker hadn't checked in with Jones for several hours.

The last time they talked was after Mrs. Tunsil visited her first shoe store. It was then that Recker figured it was going to be a long day. His hope was that whatever was on tap, that it'd happen quickly. Much to his chagrin, that didn't happen. Recker told the professor that he'd check later when something happened. Considering it'd been a while, Jones assumed nothing interesting had happened yet.

"Mike, are you there?"

"Where else would I be?"

"I take it there's been no sign of our shooter?"

Recker let out a rather loud sigh before answering. "Nope. No sign. Of anything."

Jones started to laugh, knowing how much Recker was bothered by his lack of inactivity, but quickly held it inside. "Well, something should be happening soon."

"Why? You get something?"

"No. But the initial contacts that we had indicated today was the day," Jones said. "Since it hasn't happened yet, that must mean it's getting close."

"Doesn't mean anything of the kind," Recker said in frustration. "Just means I've wasted half my day."

"We both know these situations are sometimes part of the job."

"Doesn't mean I have to like it."

"No, it doesn't. Where are you now?"

"Gas station. She's filling up. I assume she's heading home after this."

"Why would you assume that?"

"Because I think she already hit every shoe and

clothing store in the area," Recker said, obviously irritated that he hadn't come into any action yet.

This time, Jones couldn't help but let out a laugh that Recker could hear, though he still tried to hide it by holding the phone away from him.

"Something you find amusing?"

"Oh no, no, nothing. So which part is giving you the most angst. The waiting? The shoe shopping? What?"

"I can sit in this car all day if I have to. But when I have to follow someone inside a store and find myself staring at dresses and shoes, my trigger finger starts getting itchy."

"Did you find any good deals or bargains?"

"David, don't start. Comedy is not your strong suit."

"Fair enough," Jones said with a laugh.

"You still keeping tabs on the husband?"

"Still at the golf course. Just took a call on his phone a few minutes ago."

"Get a fix on who it was? Shooter maybe?" Recker said, hoping.

"Unfortunately not. It was one of his assistants at the office. I already ran it down."

"Good alibi for him. Wife gets knocked off somewhere, and he's out at the golf course with his buddies. Out in the wide open."

"Indeed. He's playing in a foursome and they'll all obviously vouch for him being there. Makes it more difficult to implicate him."

"But not impossible," Recker said.

"No. There have been several murder-for-hire cases that have made the rounds in the last few years. If they leave a trail, they can be caught. But it is more difficult. And in this instance, they've covered their tracks extremely well."

"How long's Tunsil been at the golf course?"

"Well his tee time was 2:05. The average time for an amateur foursome to play a round of golf is about four hours, sometimes a little more."

"And how far away is the course?"

"About thirty minutes."

Recker looked at the time. "He's been playing for about two hours. Means he's got two hours left."

"At least. He also may spend some time in the club-house after they're done and kick a few back."

"Even if he goes straight home after playing, he probably won't get there until seven or so, wouldn't you say?"

"Most likely. And if he does decide to stay and spend time with the boys, so to speak, then you could be looking at another hour after that."

"In any case, I'd say it's likely that whatever goes down, it'll probably happen in the next two hours."

"Could be right, but why do you think so?" Jones said.

"I have a feeling that he wants it to be done while he's on the golf course. Like squarely in the middle of the round so there's no doubt about where he's at. If he waits until after he's done, then there could always be some doubt about his location. I'm willing to bet that he wants a positive ID that he's playing golf at the time his wife is killed."

"Well my own hunch says that you are probably correct. But even if we have the time nailed down, that still leaves how out of the equation."

Recker didn't respond for a minute as he thought about how Mrs. Tunsil's death might have been arranged. "Has to be at their house."

"What leads you to that?"

"She's been gone all day and not a peep. Not a strange look or an evil glance from anybody, no one following her... other than me. If it was going to happen out in public, they've had all day to make it happen. But they haven't."

"Did you consider the possibility that maybe someone was following her, and they spotted you doing the same, and that scared them off."

"Nope."

"Why not?" Jones said.

"Because I would've noticed if someone else was following her."

"Not if they were better at it than you are."

"Did you just insult me?"

"No. Just making a statement."

"Oh. Well, I doubt anybody they would've brought in would be better at following someone than me."

"Perhaps."

"Anyway, if they wanted it done in public, they've had plenty of chances," Recker said.

"Agreed."

"Maybe they wanna make it look like a robbery gone bad."

"Well, the Tunsil's do have home security."

"David, we both know that home security systems can be easily bypassed if you know what you're doing."

"I'm well aware, Mike. But some systems do use anti-jamming countermeasures to prevent someone from blocking signals to the door and window sensors."

"And we both know that there are countermeasures to that too," Recker said.

"I know. But we don't know that the impending shooter knows them."

"We also don't know that he doesn't."

"So what do you propose?"

"If someone's at the house waiting for her, then I need to beat her there before she walks into something she can't handle. And that I can't stop."

"Where are you now? Still at the gas station?"

"Of course not. She's on the road. I'm a few cars behind her. She was filling up her car, not a tank. How long do you think it takes to gas the car up?"

Jones put his arm up in the air, waving it around as if Recker could see him flailing away. He thought about Recker's idea, that the shooter may have been at the Tunsil house, waiting for the wife to get home. It certainly made sense, though Jones wasn't that enthusiastic about Recker getting to the house ahead of time. He would have much preferred for him to wait until he got eyes on the shooter before making any kind of move. But he also knew that it might not be possible.

"So what do you want to do?" Jones finally said.

"I dunno. I'm thinking it might be best if I get to the house first and make sure nobody's there waiting for her."

"And if the place is empty?"

"Then I'll sneak my way back out. Don't act like it's my first time doing this sort of thing."

"The next question is going to be can you actually get to the house before Mrs. Tunsil does?"

"I'll be cutting it close," Recker said. "I think I can get in front of her from here. All I need is about a five-minute buffer."

"That would be great if she was still an hour away, giving you the time you need to get ahead of her. But she's only fifteen, twenty minutes away. That doesn't give you much time."

"I'll have to make it work."

Recker knew he'd have to take a shortcut if he was going to beat Mrs. Tunsil back to her home. At least what he hoped was a shortcut. As they drove through some of the one-lane streets of Philadelphia, there was no chance for Recker to speed around her. He'd have to take a turn somewhere and hope that did the trick. He took the next right, sped down the street, and turned left at the next light. He put his foot on the gas, but with traffic, he could only go so fast. After five minutes of stop and go traffic, it was clear to Recker that he wasn't going to beat Mrs. Tunsil home. He let Jones know he was going to have to scrap his plan.

"There's no way I'm going to get there first," Recker said. "Not with all this traffic. I can't even go fifty feet without stopping or slowing down."

"You're getting into rush hour traffic."

"I'm gonna have to improvise when I get there."

"What did you have in mind?"

"I'm not sure yet. This might be a time for Detective Scarborough to make an appearance."

"I've noticed you've been leaning on him more and more lately it seems," Jones said.

"Just when it seems like it's the best option. Have something better?"

Jones thought for a minute, though he couldn't think of anything else. "No."

Recker's new hope was that he'd at least get there around the same time as Mrs. Tunsil. If he got there even five minutes after her, it might be too late. That would potentially give the shooter all the time he needed to do the job and get away as Recker fought with traffic. When he got to Lombard Street, Recker could see that he was too late. Hopefully, not fatally so. He saw Mrs. Tunsil's car parked in front of the house, and saw her getting out of her black Mercedes. Recker quickly found a parking space and hurried over to her place, knocking hard on the front door, hoping she hadn't gotten too far inside yet. To his delight, Mrs. Tunsil answered almost immediately. As she opened the door, Recker could see that she hadn't settled in yet. She still had her purse in one hand and a stack full of mail in the other.

"Can I help you?"

As he so often had done before, Recker pulled out his badge and showed it to her. "Detective Scarborough, ma'am."

A concerned look fell over the woman's face, not thinking of any possible reason that the police would be there for. "What's this about?"

"I need to search inside your home."

"What for? Do you have a warrant? What are you looking for?"

"No, it's not for you. You're not in trouble with us. We're trying to help you. We have information that your life may be in danger."

"My life? What?"

"We've got information from a confidential source that your husband has hired a contract killer to take you out," Recker said, not beating around the bush.

"What? That's crazy."

"You and your husband are going through difficult times right now, correct?"

Mrs. Tunsil hesitated slightly before answering. "Yes."

"You're almost at the stage of filing for divorce, right?"

"Yes," she said again, wondering how he knew all this.

"Your husband is concerned that a divorce is going to be costlier than just taking you out. That's why he's out playing golf right now. To give himself an alibi."

Mrs. Tunsil didn't answer, looking like she was in shock. She was in her early forties and the Tunsils had been married for fifteen years. Though they'd had their ups and downs like any married couple would, she couldn't believe that her husband would go to this length to get rid of her, just to avoid divorce payments. Recker could see that she was having trouble processing what he just told her. It was understandable, he thought. If someone had told him that somebody was trying to kill him, he wouldn't bat an eyelash or even give it a second thought. This type of life was second nature for him. He was used to it. But nobody that was normal would hear that and immediately be OK with it.

"I know it's a little bit of a shock," Recker said. "We've

been following you all day because we didn't know when the hit was supposed to happen."

"All day?"

"We got word that it was supposed to happen today. We just didn't know a time. With your husband playing golf, it makes sense that it'll happen now. I believe it might be possible that someone's waiting inside your home for you."

Mrs. Tunsil stepped to the side and turned her head around, looking at the inside of her home. She had that scary feeling that someone was behind her, the way someone does when they're watching a horror movie that frightens them into thinking someone else is next to them. Even though she initially had trouble fathoming that her husband would want her dead, after she took a minute to think about it, she realized it wasn't outside the realm of possibility. Their marriage had been careening down a dark path for a few years now. She long suspected that her husband had been having an affair for at least the last year and their arguments were getting longer and more spirited as time moved on. Now that she thought about it, a few things that Mr. Tunsil had previously told her, now made sense. An argument they had several weeks ago, the last time she mentioned the word divorce, her husband made a comment in passing that he'd kill her before he ever gave her any money in a settlement. At the time, she didn't pay much attention to it. She thought it was just one of those things that sometimes got said in a heated moment when people couldn't control their emotions. Up until now, she never even considered that he might have actually meant it. But now that there was a man at her door, telling her these unbelievable things, it would seem that it was believable indeed.

"What do you need me to do?" she solemnly said.

"Just step aside and let me comb through the house to make sure nobody else is here."

"We have a security system. Wouldn't that go off if someone was here?"

"If he's a professional then it's a good chance he knows how to bypass it," Recker said. "Pros know how to do it."

"Oh. Is it just you? Do you have a team with you?"

"No, just me for now. The rest of the squad will be on the way if I find something."

"OK. Umm, what should I do? Wait outside or something?"

"No. If he's not in here, then he could be out there waiting for you. I don't want to chance sending you out there. Do you have somewhere in here you can hide? A bathroom or closet or something?"

"There's a closet here in the hallway," she said, pointing to it.

Recker stepped inside and closed the door behind him. He took his gun out and walked over to the closet, opening the white bi-fold doors, and checking inside. With it being clear he motioned for Mrs. Tunsil to come over to him. It was a decent-sized closet, one that she wouldn't be cramped up in as she waited.

"I want you to get in there and wait for me."

"For how long?"

"Until I get you. No matter what you hear, do not come out under any circumstances, OK?"

Mrs. Tunsil nodded in agreement, though she was becoming more rattled by the second, evidenced by the fact that she now seemed to be shaking.

"Just try to take it easy," Recker said, seeing that she was more upset. "I won't let anything happen to you. Just sit in the corner there and wait until this is over. When I'm done, I'll tap on the door and call you, so you know it's me."

"OK."

With Mrs. Tunsil taken care of for the moment, Recker then started sweeping his way through the house. It was a three-story home, with the kitchen, living room and a bathroom on the main floor, bedrooms, and additional bathrooms on floors two and three. As Recker started searching through the house, he also looked for signs of entry from an intruder. An open or broken window, something that seemed out of place, anything that looked unusual. After clearing the first floor, Recker went up the spiral staircase to the second floor.

He looked in the bathroom first before moving on to the bedrooms. He searched through the first bedroom without any signs of an intruder. He then moved on to the second bedroom. He opened the door slowly, ready to fire quickly if the need arose. As he stepped inside the room, it seemed quiet. Recker looked over to the window and made an alarming discovery. The window was open. Only about a quarter of an inch. But it was enough to signal to Recker that perhaps someone recently made their way through it and was waiting in there somewhere. Of course, it didn't mean they were in that specific room. That could have just been the entry point, and they relocated to a more favorable spot. That window did overlook the back of the property, which obviously made it a more suitable place to enter the home.

Recker quickly scanned the room for where the shooter would have likely been hiding. There were only two spots that he could have been. Either under the bed or inside the walk-in closet. The rest of the room was open. There was a chair, a desk, and a dresser, but they were all flush against the wall, giving no room for someone to be behind them. Recker dropped on all fours to the carpet as he looked under the bed. With that being clear, he cautiously walked over to the closet, clinging to the wall to try to remain out of sight and out of the line of fire if someone was in there.

Standing next to the closet, Recker let out a sigh as he readied himself. He gently put his left hand on the handle of the door and brought his right hand in front of his chest, ready to fire his gun if necessary. He quickly jolted it open and stepped in the frame of the door. Almost immediately, he was met with a fist that knocked him on his back as the gun slipped out of his fingers and onto the carpet a few feet away. As he shook off the blow, he saw a man standing in front of him, pointing a gun down on him. Moving fast, before the shooter had a chance to pull the trigger, Recker kicked the gun out of the man's hand. Recker got back to his feet before the shooter had a chance to pull out another weapon. The two then exchanged punches for several minutes, neither of whom seemed to be getting a clear upper hand.

The two men rolled around the floor, wrestling for superiority, though neither got it. Once they got back to their feet, they flung each other across the bed as they each tried to bludgeon the other one with punches. It was a give and take battle for a few more minutes. As they grappled with each other, the other man got the upper hand momentarily and got Recker on the ground. As he laid flat on his back, the man put his hands around Recker's neck, trying to choke the life out of him. Recker exerted a great deal of effort to break free of the man's grasp, but was having trouble doing so. As he struggled to breathe, he writhed around, knocking into an end table alongside the bed. A glass tumbled over and fell onto the floor. Recker alertly grabbed it and smashed it on the side of his attacker's face, successfully ending the man's hold over his neck, and sending him crashing onto the floor next to him.

Recker stumbled to his feet and delivered another punch to the side of the man's face, keeping him on the ground as he thought of his next maneuver. He looked around, seeing a lamp on the same table that the glass just fell from. He walked over to it and picked it up. Recker then went over to his opponent, who was starting to get to his feet, and took a healthy swing at the man's head with the lamp. The man instantly dropped to the ground once more, blood pouring down his face from a cut on his forehead. Somehow, he wasn't knocked out from the blow, though he was extremely dazed.

Recker tossed the lamp on the ground, then put his foot on it, as he grabbed hold of the cord, yanking it free from its former host. Recker wrapped the cord around the palms of his hand as he walked around his upcoming victim. As the man struggled to get to his feet, Recker put the cord over the man's face until it nestled against the skin of his neck. As the man put his hands up to his neck to try to wrestle himself free, Recker cinched back, strengthening his grip on it. As the man was severely battered and injured, he couldn't muster up the strength or energy to free himself from Recker's grasp. As Recker leaned back, both men fell hard on the floor, though Recker didn't let up on his stranglehold. The man frantically waved his arms around, trying desperately to get the cord away from his neck before he permanently passed out. Slowly, the man's efforts became less chaotic, and it was obvious that he was losing the battle. Soon after that he stopped struggling as his arms, along with the rest of his body, went limp.

Once he was sure that the man was definitely dead, Recker finally released his grip on the cord, letting the man's body slump onto the floor. He got to his feet and checked the man's pulse, making sure he was no longer a threat. He wasn't. He was a hundred percent dead. Still feeling the effects of the long, hard-fought struggle with the hit man, Recker stumbled across the room to pick up his gun. After putting it away, he pulled out his phone and walked over to the dead man, snapping a picture of his face. He sent the picture as an attachment to Jones, hoping he could identify who it was. Not that it really changed anything, but Recker would have liked to have known a name to attach to the body. Just to wrap things up completely.

"He lost," Recker said in the text, accompanying the picture. "Find a name to go with him."

"Will do," Jones replied. "Have Mrs. Tunsil check her email. The evidence will be there."

"Got it."

With his work there done, Recker exited the bedroom and walked down the steps to the main floor. He went into the hallway near the front door where the closet was and tapped on it, letting Mrs. Tunsil know it was him, just as he said he would. He opened the bi-fold doors and saw her sitting on the floor in the corner, a few clothes draped over her lap. She still appeared frightened and looked like she was fighting back tears. Recker reached his hand out to take hers, helping her to her feet. He led her out of the closet and into the hallway as he explained what happened.

"It's over," Recker said.

"It is? Like, for good?"

"So there was a man up there waiting."

Mrs. Tunsil gaped at him, then put her hand over her mouth to try to control her emotions. "Is he gone?"

"Uh, in a way. He's dead."

"Oh my."

"We had a bit of a struggle up there. Luckily, I wound up on top."

"Umm, where is he?"

"In one of the bedrooms on the second floor," Recker said. "Don't go up and look. It's not a pretty sight."

"OK. So what now?"

"Police will be here soon."

"I thought you were the police," she said.

"No, more like a concerned third party. Stay clear of your husband until he's safely locked up."

"I don't understand…"

Recker interrupted before she could go further, seeing that she was having a hard time processing everything. "They call me The Silencer. I help people out of bad situations. As soon as I leave, log into your email. You'll find some evidence that implicates your husband in this. Show it to the police when they get here."

"I can't believe this is happening. Umm, OK, how long until they arrive?"

"Should be about five minutes."

Mrs. Tunsil rubbed her hands together as she tried to wipe the sweat off them. "I guess… thank you. For everything."

Recker grabbed her hands and held them together for a few seconds, helping them to stop from trembling. He tried to give her a reassuring smile, knowing it was a lot for her to take in. She closed her eyes and took a few deep breaths. She tried to smile to prevent some tears from flowing. After a minute, she nodded, letting him know that she was going to be OK.

"Well, I have to be going," Recker said. "The police don't usually like me interfering like this."

"Oh, um, do I tell them you were here? Or do I make something up?"

Recker smiled at her, appreciating the question. "No, just tell them everything exactly how it went down. Except me showing you the badge. That kind of helps me do these types of things."

"I'll leave that out," she said.

"You take care, all right? And the next time you get married… make sure you pick a better guy."

_____

7

When Recker got back to the office, he looked like a tired man. Like a boxer who'd just gone twelve rounds and came out with a decision victory. But at least he was the last man standing. He was the one who could put his arm up in triumph. He took a little longer to get back than usual, taking some extra time to freshen up and mentally right himself after his long day and grueling battle. When he did show himself, Jones had some news for him.

"Well, I've seen you looking worse," Jones said, observing the cuts and bruises on his friend's face.

"Should've seen the other guy."

"I did. And I also identified him. His name was Marcel Lafleur, a Canadian citizen. He has quite the background."

"Professional?"

"To say the least. Former member of the Canadian Armed Forces. After that, started freelancing and hiring out his services to the highest bidder. He's thought to be connected to at least five murders, and probably more, though there's no concrete evidence that links him to them. He's very good at what he does."

"He was."

Jones continued typing away, moving his focus away from Lafleur and onto Jared Rizzo, the suspect that Haley was waiting on. Though Recker was beat up and tired, he still offered to help out on the other assignment. He wasn't yet used to slowing down and letting someone else take over.

"Sit down, take it easy," Jones said, insisting. "Remember, that's why we got him."

"Yeah, but why let him do something on his own if I can help?"

"Mike, relax. He helped you take down several violent and armed criminals. I think he can handle one man who isn't known to be as ruthless as the others."

"Kinda hard I guess," Recker said.

"What is?"

"Sitting on the sidelines and watching someone else do what you've been doing for the last few years."

"It's for your benefit," Jones said, still typing away. "Not only yours, but the city's, the people that need help. It also means you won't feel so stretched thin. You'll be able to stay fresher, do more things."

"I know all that. It's just… different. I'll adjust to it at some point. I've just never been someone who stands back and lets someone else do the dirty work."

Jones stopped typing and looked at his partner and nodded, knowing it was difficult for him to watch someone else do the things he used to do by himself. "So how do you propose explaining your face to Mia?"

"What do you mean? What's the matter with it?"

"Well you've got a cut above your eye, some bruising around it, a cut on the bridge of your nose, a bruise on your forehead, and a bruise on your cheek."

Recker looked at him dumbfounded, still not sure what he was getting at. "Why do I need to explain something?"

"You don't think she's going to see your face like that and expect you to explain what happened to it? That's what girlfriends, and wives do..."

Recker quickly and eagerly interrupted, wanting to make sure Jones didn't get out of hand with anything. "Wife? Hold on there, Skippy. Things are going good between us, but nobody's mentioned the m word yet."

"I realize it's a little bit of a sore spot with you and you don't want people thinking that you're going soft."

"I'm not going soft," Recker said.

"I know that. I didn't say that ..."

Recker interrupted again, wanting to make sure he got his point across. "Just because I may have hung a curtain or two in the past few months, or washed some dishes or something, doesn't mean I'm any different than I was before."

Jones could see that he hit a sore spot with him. It was obvious to him that it was something that Recker had thought of before he even brought it up. Perhaps it was a side conversation Recker had with Mia, or maybe it was just something that Recker thought of on his own, afraid that people would think his domestication would interfere with his profession. Jones, though, knew that wasn't the case. Though it was obvious that Recker had indeed changed, he was happier, not as brooding, but Jones did not notice any difference in his work habits. He was still the same guy that he'd always been.

"If you've calmed yourself down now, I can finish my thought," Jones said.

Recker sighed, thinking Jones was about to say something that would annoy him. Jones' only thoughts, though, were to reinforce to Recker that even though he seemed to be unchanged professionally, he now had to be somewhat sympathetic and caring to Mia's thoughts and feelings. At least if he wanted the relationship to continue.

"What I was about to say is... that girlfriends tend to worry, especially when they see their boyfriend walking through the door with cuts and bruises on his face."

"I know that," Recker said.

"Well, how do you propose to handle that? Tell her the truth about what happened, or just ignore it completely? Or better yet, lie and tell her something else."

"What, like I fell down the steps from the office or something? Dropped my keys and the car door slammed in my face? Something like that?"

Jones raised his eyebrows, thinking those explanations were going a little toward the extreme side. Recker thought about it for another minute, wondering what Jones was getting at, still not sure what his point was. Silence filled the room, though it was not one of those uncomfortable silences. The two were close enough by that point that talking was sometimes an afterthought.

"So why do you wanna know what I'll tell Mia?"

"No specific reason," Jones said. "I was just curious."

"Oh. Well, I wasn't really planning on saying anything. Just one of those days."

"And you think that will go over well?"

"She's seen me with cuts and bruises before? Heck, she's seen me shot and bleeding."

"Yes, but that was well before you two were officially an item. Things are different when you're actually in the type of relationship you're now in. Things change."

"Why are you so interested?"

Jones snickered, not having any ulterior motive for his worries. "I'm just concerned about you as a friend, as a friend of Mia's, hoping you don't do something that would make things more difficult for you both."

"Such as?"

"Like not recognizing that telling her the truth is the best medicine you can give her, regardless of how hard it may be, or whether that truth would make her unhappy."

"So in your own sweet way, you're saying that I should tell her I was in close-quarter combat with a Canadian assassin, and that's where the cuts and bruises came from?"

"Yes."

"And you don't think that will provoke a longer discussion?"

"Mia's a very intelligent woman, Mike."

"I'm aware."

"And as such, whether you tell her the truth or not, she's likely to guess at what happened, anyway. And if she does, do you want to plant little seeds in her mind that you don't tell her the truth? When you plant a seed, it always grows into something bigger. If she assumes what happened, and you don't tell her, don't you think she will wonder what else you're not telling her?"

"Do I have to tell her every time I go to the bathroom too?" Recker said sarcastically.

Jones rolled his eyes. "Do as you wish. Girlfriends and significant others worry. It's just what they do. I like seeing you happy and hope that you can continue that way. Just some friendly advice."

Their friendly banter was interrupted by the sound of Jones' phone ringing. "It's Chris," Jones said. He answered it, putting it on speaker. "Everything OK?"

"Yeah, still no sign of Rizzo yet," Haley said. "I was just wondering how Mike made out? You told me earlier he was gonna try to find the shooter in the home."

"Oh. Yes. Mike is back, he's fine, a few bumps and bruises, but otherwise OK. The shooter's been termi-nated. All is good on that front. Mike will be back home tonight getting some TLC from his girlfriend, I'm sure."

Recker turned his head slowly to look at his partner, not believing what he just said. For the first few years that they'd known each other, Jones had a very dry personal-ity, and hardly ever seemed to crack a joke. Now they seemed to come out of his mouth constantly. Especially when it concerned Recker's love life. It didn't really bother him, though sometimes he made it appear that it did, just to keep up his tough guy front. Jones looked up at Recker and grinned, shrugging his shoulders.

"Need some help out there, Chris?" Recker said.

"No, no, no. I'm good. Just gets a little boring out here, waiting."

"I know the feeling."

"Chris, anytime you feel the need to talk, I'm always here and available," Jones said.

"Good to know. Still no word on when Rizzo might hit?" Haley said.

"No, just said after dark. That could be 8pm or 5am. Just have to wait it out and see."

Though Haley wasn't ecstatic about waiting, it didn't bother him too much. He knew it was sometimes part of the deal. He was just happy to be back in the game. For him, waiting six hours in a car was better than working five minutes at a normal job. It was a good attitude for him to have, considering he'd have another four hours to go until his suspect showed up.

It was 11:30 and the homeowners, judging from when the lights went out, went to bed around nine. Haley saw a person walking down the street and immediately looked at his phone for Rizzo's picture to get a confirmation. As he walked under a streetlight, Rizzo's face was illuminated and Haley could definitely make him out despite his dark clothing. Haley didn't take his eyes off his target as Rizzo approached the house. Rizzo stopped and looked around, making sure nobody was watching. Haley was parked across the street, in the back seat of his new car, the tinted window disguising his presence.

Once Rizzo was sure that prying eyes weren't gazing down upon him, he started to work. The row home had a walk-out basement, and Rizzo snuck up to the door that led inside. He quietly broke open the door within a minute and was inside the home. As soon as he vanished from sight, Haley exited his car and ran across the street, ready to do his business. He stood just beyond the door and peeked inside, not immediately seeing Rizzo. Haley withdrew his gun and stepped inside the house. He stood inside the frame of the door, looking around, trying to hear where the intruder might have been. After a few moments, he heard some rattling coming from the back of the house. The basement had been separated into two rooms. Where Haley was had been turned into a TV room, along with a computer, a couch, a chair, as well as a bathroom. The steps that led up to the main part of the house separated the two rooms. The part Rizzo was in had been converted into a toy room. It also led to the backyard as well as housing the washer and dryer.

Haley quietly walked to the middle of the room, near the steps, and waited for Rizzo to show himself. He figured it was safer for him to wait for Rizzo to come to him instead of him going into a room, not knowing exactly where he was. In what felt like an hour, though was actually only two minutes, Rizzo came out of the room, holding several items that he planned on stealing. Haley had his gun out, pointed at him as he came into view. As soon as Rizzo saw the outline of the gun-toting man in front of him, he knew he was in a lot of trouble. He just dropped the items in his hand without saying a word.

"I don't believe those are yours," Haley said.

"Umm," Rizzo said, throwing his arms in the air, not knowing what else to say. What else could he say? He'd been caught red-handed.

"C'mon."

With his gun, Haley pointed to the other room, having Rizzo follow him in there as he walked backward. He still wasn't sure exactly what he was going to do with the burglar. If Recker was there, it likely would have been over by now. There was a good chance he would have pumped a couple rounds into him and left to be done with it. But that wasn't Haley's style. While he obviously didn't have a problem firing away and killing someone if the situation warranted, as the Tresselman case showed, it never was his first option.

"You got any weapons on you?" Haley said. "Gun, knife, anything?"

"Nah," Rizzo said solemnly. He looked very worried about what the man with the gun was going to do with him.

Haley turned him around and had him face the wall and touch it, spreading out his hands and feet. Haley frisked him to make sure he had no weapons, but as Rizzo admitted, he was clean.

"Just stay there for a second," Haley said.

Haley took a few steps back and started looking around the room. He still kept his gun on Rizzo and looked back at him every few seconds, just to make sure he didn't make any sudden movements or try escaping somehow. There wasn't a lot that he could do with the burglar. He wasn't going to kill him or beat him up. Especially since the man had seemingly given up peacefully. Rizzo didn't make any attempts to get away or attack him. Haley could have tied him up, but he obviously didn't walk around with a string of rope hanging off him, and he didn't notice anything he could use in the basement. Haley noticed a closet and figured that would have to do. He directed Rizzo to move away from the wall and had him move closer to the door. Haley opened the closet, hoping it wasn't already filled with junk that would spill out as soon as he opened it. Luckily, there were only a few small things in there. Haley lifted his thumb and pointed at the closet with it.

"I gotta go in there?" Rizzo asked, hoping that wasn't the case.

"It's either that or I can shoot you."

Rizzo sighed in disgust, but complied with the request, knowing there wasn't much he could do to stop it. As his record indicated, he wasn't a violent man by nature. Though he was a criminal, and burglary was one of his specialties, he wasn't prone to outbursts of violence. He'd never shot anyone before and he tried to shy away from physical confrontations whenever possible. He knew that once he stepped inside that closet that the next time it opened, there would probably be a police officer on the other side of it, ready to take him to jail.

"That thing even loaded?" Rizzo said.

"One good way to find out," Haley said with a certain vigor in his voice.

The manner in which he said it indicated to Rizzo that the man wasn't fooling around. He certainly looked like someone who knew his way around with a gun. Considering Rizzo wasn't exactly a gun aficionado, he wasn't the type to question anyone else's motives who was carrying one. Reluctantly, Rizzo finally stepped inside the closet. Haley immediately closed it and locked it. To make sure the burglar didn't escape once he left, Haley took hold of the computer desk and dragged it across the floor until it set in front of the door to prevent it from opening. Not completely satisfied with the setup, Haley looked around the floor for any other items he could use. He saw a milk crate on the floor that was packed with books and picked it up. He placed the heavy object under the desk, nestling it in front of the door. Once Haley was sure that Rizzo couldn't get away, even if he could unlock the door, he called Jones to let him know the job was done and seek further clarification on what to do from there.

"Everything's wrapped up here," Haley said. "Rizzo's under control."

"Great. What did you do with him?" Jones said, a slight hesitation in his voice. Usually when he asked that question of Recker it involved hearing about a dead body. Whether Jones thought it was warranted or not. He hoped that this wouldn't be another of those times. Especially with Haley.

"Right now he's locked in a closet in the basement."

"Oh."

"Is that wrong? Should I not have done that?" Haley said, noticing the apprehensiveness in Jones' voice.

"No. No. What you did was perfect. I take it he did not give you any trouble?"

"Nope. Easy as pie. As soon as he saw me he dropped the stuff and pretty much gave up. No struggle at all."

"Excellent. Great job."

"I didn't know exactly what else to do with him, so I

figured stuffing him in the closet was the best option. I didn't have anything to tie him up with."

"Is the closet secured?" Jones said, hoping Rizzo wouldn't get loose once Haley left the premises.

"Yeah. I locked it and put a desk and a crate of heavy books in front of it. I mean, he may be able to pry himself out of there eventually, but it should take a while."

"I'll contact the police immediately. They should be there in a few minutes."

"Yeah, he won't be able to get out in that time."

"OK. After we hang up, wait approximately thirty seconds, then get out of there."

"Will do."

Haley did exactly as he was instructed and left thirty seconds after talking to Jones. Even though he was sure that Jones wanted him to leave the area right away, Haley stuck around for a little while. He wanted to make sure that Rizzo didn't somehow escape before the police got there. Haley did move his car to a new position, though, just to be out of the sight of any police personnel that would soon swamp the area. He moved a little farther down the street, but he still had a good sight line of the home and could see if Rizzo came out before the police came.

Jones, meanwhile, had already called the police anonymously to report seeing a burglar in the home. He made sure to tell them it was urgent, and the burglar was still in the house. He tried to monitor the situation remotely as he listened to police scanners. The police showed up within only a few minutes. Even after they arrived, Haley stayed until he saw them leading Rizzo out of the house in handcuffs. Once they did, he gave Jones the heads-up that the case was now closed. He was about to go back to the office to wrap things up, but Jones nixed that idea and told him to go home instead. With everything settled, Jones was about to call it a night himself.

Haley was just looking to learn as much as he could about the new operation he'd found himself in. There was still so much that he didn't know. Jones and Recker had given him bits and pieces of information and showed him a few things, but he didn't completely understand the nuts and bolts of the business. Wanting to get a head start, Haley showed up at the office at 8 a.m. the next morning, hoping he might be the first one there. He was a little taken aback, though not completely surprised, to find that he was actually the last one in the office. It didn't appear that they'd yet actually started working as they were both standing near the coffee machine. After a brief greeting from his new teammates, Haley got a cup of coffee himself.

"And here I thought I might actually beat everyone in," Haley said.

"Not likely," Recker said with a laugh. "Better get used to it. In the few years we've been doing this, I can count on one hand the amount of times I beat David into the office. It just isn't gonna happen."

"I pride myself on being first to distribute any infor-mation that may be necessary to start the day," Jones said.

"And it's gonna be even harder now that he's living here and doesn't have a separate place."

Jones took a sip of his coffee before asking Recker

how his night went. "So how did you handle the topic of your battered and bruised face?"

Recker shrugged and shook his head like it was no big deal. "Just told her the truth. Told her exactly what happened."

"You left nothing out?"

"Not one detail."

"And how did she take it?" Jones said, though considering his friend didn't seem upset or troubled, he already assumed it went reasonably well.

"Fine. Like you said, she did the girlfriend worrying thing, but we talked about it."

"Who did most of the talking?"

"She did. But she knows this is what I do, and we've talked about it before. It isn't going to change anytime soon. She's dealing with it. She's a strong person though."

"Sounds like a great girl," Haley said.

"She is," Recker said. "I probably don't deserve her."

"Probably not," Jones said, getting an icy stare from Recker. "What? Well, I was only agreeing."

"So how's your apartment coming? All settled in?" Recker said.

Haley laughed as he thought about it. "Well, there's a TV, a couch, a bed, and a dining table. That's pretty much it."

"Sounds like you could use an interior decorator," Jones said. "Mike, you should help him with that. He knows all about hanging curtains, don't you?"

Recker looked up at the top of the wall and the ceiling, stroking his chin as he tried to figure out whether he should respond to the teasing. After a few moments of thought, he decided to just let it go. "If you want, one day Mia and I can come over and help you spruce the place up. Well, she'll most likely do most of the work. I just pretty much just stand back and do what she tells me."

"That would be great if you think she wouldn't mind," Haley said. "I wouldn't want to impose on her or anything."

"Nah, she'd love to do it. She loves doing that kind of stuff. Besides, she's already been asking me to meet you."

"Oh, really?"

"Yeah, she's hopeful that your being here is going to magically add years to my life."

8

Recker and Haley had just come back from a rather routine assignment, preventing a simple assault on a man who was responsible for a couple of his ex-coworkers being fired. The man was a retail store manager and had recently fired two of his employees for stealing merchandise. The employees had planned on getting back at the man by beating him up one night as he closed the store and walked back to his car. Recker and Haley easily stopped that, leaving the two assailants down and out before they could get a hand on their intended victim. They planned on keeping an eye on the situation in the coming weeks, but after the beating that Recker and Haley dished out, they suspected they would never hear from the pair again.

By coming back to the office later at night, Recker knew something was up. Usually when they had something go down past nine o'clock, they just called it a night and reconvened the next morning. Since Jones had asked them to come back after their assignment was over,

Recker assumed there was another case coming. And probably coming immediately.

"Any issues?" Jones said.

"No, it's taken care of," Recker said. "I doubt we'll hear from either of them again. Couple of small-time punks who thought it'd be an easy thumping for them."

"They are still breathing, correct?"

"What do you take me for, an animal?"

"Just making sure."

"Alive, breathing, and going home to mama."

"Though they'll have some cuts and bruises to take care of," Haley said. "Maybe a few stitches too."

"So what's up?" Recker said. "I know you didn't call us back here just to chat about these two nitwits."

"I received a warning on the voicemail alert system," Jones said quickly.

"What's the target?"

"Liquor store. Store's open until ten. The message said they were going to hit it just before closing."

"How far away?"

"If you leave now, you'll get there about the same time they do."

"How many are we dealing with?"

"Four. And they're not afraid of using their weapons," Jones said, pulling up the gang's information on the screen.

It showed a picture of all four of the men along with their rap sheets. Recker and Haley both leaned forward, each standing on opposite sides of Jones, looking over his shoulders to read as much as they could before they got going.

"I believe this might be the same gang that hit that liquor store a few weeks ago that we rolled on late to," Jones said.

"What happened with that?" Haley said.

"Same thing. They walked into the store just before closing, then took everything out of the registers and the safe. Killed an employee and a customer on their way out," Recker said, remembering the details vividly.

"Was there provocation?" Haley asked, wondering what made the gang take the lives of two people.

"Not according to witnesses," Jones said. "Everyone was apparently complying to their wishes and demands without incident. The gang just seemed to open up on the victims for no reason at all."

"The same guy do the shooting?"

"No, it was two different shooters."

"I don't see a vehicle listed," Recker said.

"I'm still working on that," Jones replied. "If I get it before you arrive at the store I'll let you know."

"Forward it to our phones so we can look at it on the way."

"We both hitting this?" Haley said.

"You know it," Recker said, confirming the obvious.

Recker and Haley then rushed out of the office. Since Recker was more familiar with the area, he did the driving. They jumped into his SUV and Recker floored it to get to the liquor store on time. As they sped through the streets, Jones sent the information on the gang, complete with pictures, to the phones of both Recker and Haley. Haley immediately started studying their faces and looked at their histories and background info.

Though he had no issue with taking on the gang themselves, he did have some questions on the assignment.

"Why not just call the police and let them know what's going on and let them roll on it?" Haley said.

Recker sighed, not annoyed with the question, but reliving what happened the last time this situation happened. "Because when this happened a few weeks ago, that's how we handled it."

"Police didn't help?"

"Not in time. We called in the tip and by the time they got there, the gang had already come and gone. We took too long on it. We debated back and forth on whether to get the police involved or just handle it ourselves. After we got the police involved I eventually rolled on it, but I didn't get there fast enough."

"That's rough."

"We should've just handled it ourselves," Recker said, shaking his head, still lamenting their lack of action at the time.

"No alarms went off?"

"No. That was one of the things we talked about. We assumed that one of the workers would hit the silent alarm when the robbery went down. We waffled on whether, if the alarm was sounded, if I would get caught up in between the gang and the police. If I kept them pinned down, or they kept me pinned down, could I slip away if the cops showed?"

"Reasonable worry," Haley said.

"Yeah, well, turns out the cops got there late, I got there late, the store got robbed, and two people got killed because of it."

"So how we gonna handle it?"

"I guess that will depend on if they're already there or not. Hopefully, we can get there before they do, and we can already be inside waiting on them. If not, we may have to shoot our way in. Or catch them as they're leaving."

"Might be too late, though. Especially if they shoot a couple people before they head out the door and we see them," Haley said.

Recker nodded, instead, only answering with a grimace. He was well aware that their best chance of stopping the gang was to get inside of the store before they did. If not, they'd most likely have to shoot their way in, and that would only endanger more innocent people's lives. The more Recker agonized over it, the more determined he was to not let the same thing happen again that happened a few weeks ago.

When they were about ten minutes away from their destination, Jones texted them with the make and model of the car that he suspected the gang was driving. It was a plain blue cargo van with a New Jersey license plate. Now it was always possible that they could be using a different car, or had stolen something new along the way, but according to what Jones could dig up, the cargo van was their likely choice of a getaway car. They kept a sharp lookout for the van when they finally arrived at the liquor store, which was in a small shopping center. There weren't a ton of parking spots and few places for it to hide if they were keeping it parked out of sight. Recker went through the lot, and even drove behind the buildings, in case they were waiting in back of the stores. Much to their delight, the van was nowhere in sight. But that still didn't mean that they weren't there. There were a few cars parked along the side of the building, and since the liquor store was an end unit, they assumed they were the cars of the store workers. They pulled up alongside them and shined their flashlight inside the cars one by one to make sure the gang wasn't inside one of them waiting to strike. Each of the four cars came up empty though. Not a single passenger in any of them.

Recker pulled the truck around to the front of the building again and parked. They made what they believed was a safe assumption that the gang wasn't there yet. If the car they were using wasn't to the side of the building, they figured it would've been parked near the front entrance along the curb. Parking in a regular spot would not have been conducive to a fast getaway should they need it. Recker and Haley waited a few seconds, looking into the store from the spot they were parked in. They could easily see a few workers walking around freely and two or three customers shopping.

"Time to head in?" Haley said.

"Yeah."

"How you wanna work it? Alert the workers that they're about to be hit?"

"Nah, I don't think that'd play well," Recker said, nixing the idea. "We go in there and start talking about getting robbed, talking crazy, they're likely to hit the panic button right away and not even let us finish a coherent thought. Next thing you know, instead of the gang showing up, we got a bunch of police officers waiting for us outside."

"All right, makes sense. Light these guys up as soon as they walk through the door?"

"I dunno. I think we gotta play it by ear. I wanna get all four of them. If only two enter and we kill them right away, the other two might rabbit."

"Might scare the rest of them off," Haley said.

"Or it might just make them come back in a week or two. Maybe even worse or more dangerous than before. A wounded animal is a dangerous animal. And I'd rather take out this entire crew now than worrying about having to deal with them again somewhere down the line."

Recker and Haley got out of the car and walked into the store. There was still ten minutes before closing. Plenty of time for the gang to storm in and do their business. Recker split from his partner as they both pretended to be customers, each walking a different aisle of the store, perusing the selection of alcohol. They both stayed within viewing range of the entrance, so they could be ready to strike quickly if needed. Five minutes passed, with still no sign of any activity from the gang. Two of the customers did leave, however, and no other shoppers entered, which pleased Recker. It meant two fewer people who would be in the line of fire.

With two minutes to go until the store closed, two rough looking characters calmly walked through the doors. Recker took a good long look at the pair, instantly recognizing them as part of the crew they were waiting for. A closing announcement boomed over the loudspeaker, trying to speed up the selection process of any remaining customers. The first two members of the crew split up, walking toward the back of the store. Then, the other two guys came strutting through the door. One of them stayed near the front door as the other one started waltzing through the aisles. The first two members that came in had grabbed something off the shelf and headed toward the registers.

To get their plan into action, one of the men pretended there was some type of problem at the register, bringing the store manager out. With the three employees from the store all hanging around near the registers, the crew knew there was nobody else to worry about. The gang had cased the store several times over the past two weeks and were aware how the establishment operated around closing time, and how many employees there were at nighttime. They often waited for a while after it closed to see how many store workers exited when they finally closed everything down, so they knew how many people they had to worry about.

Recker maneuvered his way to the front of the store, near the entrance, where the last member of the gang was waiting to make sure nobody else went in or out. He'd already communicated with Haley to not engage until he gave him the signal. As Recker walked to the front, the man withdrew his gun to keep what he assumed was a customer at bay. Haley, meanwhile, had walked to the back of the store to get within range of the man walking the aisles. Recker's signal was going to be his gun firing, and Haley wanted to be ready to extract some justice of his own before one of the robbers could get the drop on him first.

"Get down on the floor, buddy," the man said, pointing his gun at Recker.

"Oh, sure," Recker said nonchalantly, putting his hands in the air.

Recker got to one knee, putting his right one down, trying to lull the man to sleep by being as unthreatening as possible. As Recker put one of his hands on the floor, he noticed the guard took his eyes off him for a split second as he scanned the store for anybody else within his vicinity. That was just the opening that Recker needed to get the drop on him. He quickly withdrew his gun and opened fire at the man, unloading three shots that all lodged in the man's upper torso, dropping the guard immediately. Recker scurried along the floor to check on the man's condition, wanting to make sure he was dead, so he didn't have to worry about him coming back at him from behind.

Haley was standing near the end cap of one of the aisles, waiting for the sound he needed to hear. The crackling sounds of gunfire within the store was the signal that Haley needed to engage his own target. With the second member of the crew guarding the back, Haley had his gun drawn, and jumped from beyond the protection of the aisle. Catching the man by surprise, Haley immediately opened fire, firing two rounds, both of which connected with his target. One of the bullets penetrated the side of the man's head, causing him to perish before he even hit the ground.

After checking on the status of the man he shot, Recker hurried back to the security of one of the aisles to make sure he wasn't within easy range of the two remaining members of the gang. Haley also rushed back to the front of the store, spotting Recker and racing over to him. Seeing movement out of the corner of his eye, Recker turned toward his partner zooming toward him.

"You all right?" Recker said.

"Yep."

"You take the other guy out?"

"Yeah. Just the two left," Haley said, breathing a little heavy from the action. "How you wanna do this?"

"Looks like they got the three employees up there by the register. That means there should still be a customer floating around here somewhere. See if you can find them and get them out of here."

"OK. I'll have them go through the fire exit door in back."

"Sounds good. I'll start working these guys up here."

Haley immediately left and started combing through the aisles, keeping his head down in case of a random shot being fired in his direction. After a brief search, he found the last remaining customer, kneeling, and covering his head in the middle of one of the aisles. Haley sped over to him and tried to keep the middle-aged man as calm as possible.

"Hey," Haley said calmly, putting his hand on the man's shoulder.

The man withdrew his head from his arms, looking up at the armed man with a worried expression on his face.

"Listen, I'm gonna get you out of here, OK? I'm one of the good guys. Both of the robbers are up front with the employees. What I want you to do is keep your head down and go right down to the end of this aisle and make a left. There's a fire door there. I want you to go out the door and get to your car and get out of here."

"OK." The man nodded his agreement.

"Go. Keep your head down."

The customer did as he was directed and ran to the back of the store, hunched over the entire time. As he raced out the exit door, the alarm started blaring from the door opening. As the alarm went off, Recker looked to the ceiling. He knew that meant someone would be coming soon enough. Even if none of the workers hit the emergency button, someone would probably be coming soon since the alarm company would be calling momentarily about the unauthorized door opening. Recker knew they'd have to work fast to avoid any law enforcement that might be coming, but not so quickly that they'd rush something and get one of the innocent store workers hurt or killed. Up to that point, everything had happened so fast, that the gang hadn't even gotten any money yet. None of the cash register drawers had been emptied, and they hadn't got to the safe yet. But hearing the gunshots, and seeing their friend lying dead by the front door, they knew they had to scrap their plans and just figure out how to get out of there alive. What made things tougher for them at that stage was that they couldn't see who else was in the store with them or where they were.

Finally, the crew's leader spoke up in trying to get themselves out of there. "We got three people up here. If you don't let us out of here, they'll all wind up dead."

"I'm not the police," Recker shouted back. "I don't negotiate. Letting those people go is the only chance you have of getting out of here."

"Fat chance, man."

"Listen, it's just me. But you can see how dangerous I can be. I've taken out two of your guys already. I got no problem taking out two more."

Recker wanted to play coy with them, hoping that they didn't realize there was a second shooter, or that he was working with someone. If they believed it was just him, then they might get a free shot at the gang, or at least a better opportunity to take them out. Through the com device in his ear, Recker started talking with Haley to go over the plan.

"They didn't correct me or dispute it when I told them it was just me," Recker said. "Try to get to the far side of the store to see if you can get a better angle."

"Right."

"Try not to let them see you."

"If I can get a good vantage point, should I take the shot?" Haley said.

"As long as you're sure nobody's in the way. If you're positive you can take one out... do it."

Haley steadily went to the back of the store once more, moving slowly from aisle to aisle, making sure that he didn't make any noises to alert the gang of his presence. Recker was hopeful that Haley could make his way around to the other side of the gang undetected. It would definitely speed things up if he could. If the civilians weren't there, Recker would fire a few rounds in the gang's direction, just to get them distracted. But with the workers nearby, Recker couldn't take the chance of a bullet ricocheting off a wall and hitting them.

As he waited for word from Haley that he'd gotten

himself into a better position, Recker took a moment to think about how nice it was to have some help in that situation. Before Haley was brought into the fold, Recker would've had to go about this in a completely different manner. Or in the event that he didn't, he would've had a much tougher time. If he would've had to worry about taking on all four men on his own, it was also likely that it would take a lot longer, possibly screwing up his probabilities of escaping before the police came. Even now, with Haley's help, it was a cause of concern for him.

After a couple minutes, Haley notified him that he was ready. "I'm in position."

"How's your view?"

"Uh, not as good as I'd like it to be. Looks like they're huddled down behind a couple of the registers."

"No clear shot?"

"No, not yet."

"We're gonna have to raise the target somehow," Recker said. "Gotta make them visible."

"Any ideas?"

Recker thought for a few moments before thinking he might've come up with something. "Yeah. I might."

Recker then explained his thoughts, not totally sure himself whether it was going to work. There was a risk involved. He thought they could probably take one of the men out easily, but he had no idea how the remaining member of the gang would react once they did. He could just give it up, or he could panic and start killing the civilians he had with him.

"You ready to surrender yet?" Recker yelled. "You know there's nowhere for you to go."

"We'll see about that."

Recker took a step to the side of the aisle that he was in, showing himself for a brief moment. Seeing only the tops of a couple people's heads, he took aim at the glass window that was in front of the register. Knowing that the glass would shatter, with minimal chance of injuring any of the civilians severely, Recker fired at it. He thought the people were far enough away from the glass that they shouldn't have to worry about pieces of glass raining down on top of them. But even if a few pieces did manage to strike one or two of them, they should've only produced a few minor cuts.

After the glass shattered, Recker was correct in that the people were far enough away that the pieces didn't reach them. But it did do as he hoped it would and spurred the two remaining gang members to start moving from their position. The man closest to Haley's spot rose up and started hurrying the store worker that he had with him, wanting him to move with him and use him as a hostage. The gang member grabbed the man by the back of his shirt collar, spurring him on to move along in front of him, shielding him from any bullets. They started to leave the comfort of the registers and move to the back of the store, though they only got about fifteen feet away. They passed right by Haley's position, giving the new Silencer a perfect view of his target.

Though the gang member and his hostage were relatively close to each other, there was enough separation for Haley to do what was needed. As soon as the store worker passed by, Haley had a clear shot of his target. Only a few feet away, Haley's shot penetrated the temple of the crew member, instantly knocking him onto his side. Upon hearing and seeing the carnage that was unleashed just inches behind him, the store worker froze in his position. Haley worried about him being exposed and quickly grabbed him by the arm and pulled him behind his location as they retreated back to Haley's former spot.

"You know the back exit, right?" Haley said.

"Yeah."

"All right, run, get out of here."

The worker ran as fast as he could down the aisle and swiftly made his way out the fire door in the back of the building. The last member of the gang had just risen above the confines of the register when he saw his partner start making his way to the back in the hopes of escaping. Once he saw his friend's head almost blown off his shoulders, he quickly retreated back to the register, still having the security of two hostages with him.

"Give it up," Recker shouted, hoping to bring the matter to a resolution quickly. "There's no way out for you."

"Now I know there's at least two of you," the man yelled in return. "I'm not making that mistake again."

"Doesn't really matter, does it? You know we're not letting you walk out of here with hostages."

"I'll blow their heads off right now if you don't let me out of here."

"And as I said earlier, I'm not the police. I don't negotiate."

"Well you better start, or these people are as good as dead."

Seeing as how they were at an impasse, Recker turned to Haley to see if he could sneak in behind the man. "Chris, you able to move closer?"

"Uh, maybe. Not sure."

"I think that's our best bet of ending this. He's not letting them go. We need to take him out now."

"What if he sees me coming?" Haley said.

"Do what you gotta do."

"No, I'm not concerned about me. I can handle that. I'm worried that if he sees me, he might kill one of those people he's got with him."

"Knowing what you did to his friend, I'm betting that if he sees you, he's gonna be more concerned about you than taking out one of them," Recker said.

"I can give it a shot."

"Even if you can't get to him. If we can get him to stand up, we can take him out. I can move a little closer. If you don't think you have a shot, if he stands up to face you, I can hit him from here."

The two Silencers both moved away from their current position, trying to get a little closer to the last remaining member of the gang. He still had two store workers huddled with him, crunching down beneath one of the registers. The man really didn't know what he was going to do. He had no plan at that point. All his buddies had been killed. It appeared that he was surrounded. It didn't seem like he could even leverage the store workers as hostages to buy his release. It really seemed hopeless for him. Beside that, he didn't even know who he was up against. If it was the police, he knew there was a certain guide that they followed in situations like these. But not having any idea who was on the other side, they didn't appear to be playing by any definite rules. They only seemed to be going by the idea that they had to take everyone out.

Haley dropped to the tile floor and started crawling along the side of the wall to make his way to the front register. As he was doing that, Recker also moved closer, crouching down as he maneuvered his way to the end register. The gang member was two registers away from him, and if he stood up, Recker had a clear shot at him. There was no way he'd miss at that range.

"I don't know if I can get in anymore," Haley whispered.

"It's all right. I can hit him from here," Recker said. "See if you can get him to stand up a little."

Haley thought for a moment about what he could do or say to get the man to reveal himself for Recker to finish him off. He was staring at a bottle of wine right in front of him and thought that might give them the diversion that they needed to finally end the conflict. He grabbed it off the shelf and tossed it toward the end of the register, shattering as it impacted against the ground. Thinking someone had snuck up behind him at the register, the man turned and instinctively started firing, his bullets hitting the front wall. As he did so, his head jumped up just slightly above the counter of the register, finally giving Recker a target to shoot at. Seizing the opportunity, Recker wasted no time in firing his weapon. He only needed one shot, and he didn't miss. Upon the bullet piercing through the side of his face, the man slumped over, dead as he hit the ground.

Recker got to his feet and walked over to his latest victim to make sure the situation was finally resolved. Seeing the blood pouring out of the hole in the side of his face, it was conclusive evidence that their work was now finished. Recker waved to the last two hostages to get on their feet, letting them know that the nightmare was over. As they ran to the front door to escape the carnage that was behind them, sirens blared in the background. The two workers ran right into the waiting arms of several police officers.

Recker looked out the front window and saw at least five police cars in front, the magnitude of their lights brightening up the entire area. Recker and Haley looked at each other, hoping they hadn't run out of time. Recker tapped Haley on the shoulder to get him to follow him as they raced toward the back door. Recker opened it just a bit, wanting to make sure they didn't run out into the flashing lights of police officers themselves. Unfortunately for them, there were already three cars stationed around the back. Recker looked at Haley and sighed, unsure how they were going to escape the predicament they were now in.

"What do we do?" Haley said, not seeming the least nervous about being surrounded.

"See if there's another way out. Go around the store and see if there's another exit somewhere."

"Even if there is, they're gonna be out there waiting."

Recker put his hand over his face and rubbed the sides of his mouth as he tried to think of another solution. For the first time that he could remember since starting this operation with Jones, he didn't see a way out.

At least not one that left him alive. Shooting it out was not an option. His long standing policy was to never engage the police under any circumstances since they were on the same side, and he wasn't going to change that now, even if that was the only choice he had left. A few minutes later, Haley came back to let Recker know that he struck out. There were no other possibilities.

"What about a roof hatch?" Recker said, remembering he's used that several times to escape.

"Locked and deadbolted."

Since escape was no longer on the table, the grim reality set that Recker's final minutes as a free man were coming near. There was nothing else he could do but give himself up. The only question now was how to keep Haley in the clear. If Recker was out of the picture, he couldn't let Haley get dragged down with him. Jones would still need somebody out in the field to make things work. His thoughts turned to Mia briefly, thinking how disappointed and upset he was going to make her.

"Find the office and any surveillance equipment, tapes, anything," Recker said.

"And do what with them?" Haley replied, not getting what his partner was inferring.

"Make sure nobody can ever see what went down here tonight."

"Why?"

"Cause we're going down and I'm gonna make sure you don't go down with me."

"I'm not gonna leave you high and dry," Haley said, resisting the idea he'd escape the wrath of the law while his partner got hung up.

"It's not about that. People need to be protected... helped. They won't get that if we're both in the can. I'm already a known quantity. Nobody knows about you yet. And they don't have to. As far as anyone is concerned, everything that happened here tonight was me. I stopped the gang alone. You're just a customer. Wrong place, wrong time."

Haley sighed and made a grimace, not really liking the plan that Recker was offering. Though it obviously made sense to him, he wasn't keen on just leaving his new partner and friend in the clutches of the police.

"There is no other way," Recker insisted, seeing that Haley was having a hard time swallowing his proposition. "Go hit the office and get rid of those tapes so nobody can see what role you had here."

Haley sighed even louder as he looked down at the ground, not wanting to move an inch. He raised his head up and looked at Recker and nodded, finally agreeing to his plan, though he was still reluctant to do so. Recker moved the corner of his mouth to try to muster a smile, letting him know that it was OK. As Haley left, Recker watched him as he ran toward the front office. He knew that if he was now out of the game, that Jones would still have a good man out in the field. This was as bad as it got, and Haley showed no signs of panic or worry. Even looking at the loss of freedom, he wasn't about to abandon his partner, even though it would've been easier to do so. It was an admirable quality to have, and Haley had plenty. If there was any solace to be taken from this event, it was that the work that Jones and Recker had started would still go on. Haley was a capable replacement, and once he had a little more experience, it would probably be like Recker never even left.

Recker heard someone's voice blaring through a police radio, trying to make contact with him, though he didn't pay any attention to it. Haley came back and let him know that he destroyed the surveillance equipment, so there should've been no evidence of his presence once they were gone.

"What now?" Haley said.

"First, I'll call David and let him know what's happening."

Jones was already aware of some of the problems. He'd been monitoring police communications and knew that they were already on the premises. Though he worried about Recker and Haley getting caught up in things, he hoped that they were just getting a safe distance away before contacting him to let him know how the assignment went. When Recker called to let him know the situation, it was the call that Jones had dreaded for so long, the one he hoped would never come, though he always knew would happen at some point. He just hoped it wouldn't be for a long time in the future. Seeing Recker's call come in, Jones quickly answered on the first ring.

"The police just descended on the liquor store," Jones said, hoping he was informing Recker with new information.

"I know."

"Please tell me you and Chris are already long gone."

Recker made a noise that almost sounded like a laugh, but didn't reply back instantly. It was with that lack of an immediate confirmation that Jones knew his worst fears had come true. He closed his eyes and felt like his heart had sunk as he waited for Recker to acknowledge the fact.

"Can't," Recker said, unable to say anything more profound.

"You're still inside," Jones said, barely able to get the words out.

Recker sighed. "Yeah."

"Since that's the case, I assume that there's no possible way out."

"No."

"So what do you propose to do?" Jones solemnly said.

"There's only one thing to do."

"Which is?"

"Give myself up."

"No, there must be another way."

"David, if there was, I would've taken it by now."

"I can't believe that the only way out of this is to surrender," Jones said, trying to think of another solution.

"It doesn't have to be a total loss, though," Recker said, attempting to convey some sort of positive.

"And how do you compute that?"

"Chris doesn't have to go down with me."

"You'll have to explain this further."

"We've already destroyed all the security footage. They won't be able to connect the dots with him."

"And none of the customers or store employees saw him do any of the damage?" Jones said, unsure that the plan would actually work.

"Well, he helped usher a couple of them out the back

door. I dunno, passing him off as a customer who just happened to be there seems to be the best way to get him out safely. I'm the only one they know about. He shouldn't get caught up in it."

"I just wish there was a better option."

"Believe me, so do I."

9

R ecker and Haley tossed their guns on the ground to make sure there would be no battle once they exited the store. Recker looked at Haley and smiled, giving him a pat on the arm.

"Take care of things while I'm gone," Recker said.

"We'll figure out a way to get you out."

Recker nodded, appreciating the gesture, even if he thought it was an impossible task. "Stay back. I'll go out first. I'll tell them you're a customer and you're the last one inside. Just stick with the story. Don't act like you know me at all. No matter what happens."

"I will."

With Haley looking on, Recker finally opened the front door and walked outside. With the bright lights flashing, he squinted as his feet hit the pavement.

"Get down on the ground! Get down on the ground!" someone shouted.

Recker instantly complied with the orders, getting down to his knees and putting his hands behind his head.

"That's the Silencer! Go! Go!" a police lieutenant yelled.

Within a few seconds, a dozen police officers descended on Recker's position, surrounding him as they put his hands behind his back and handcuffed him. As they got him to his feet and started walking him to one of their cars, they read him his rights.

"Anybody else inside?" an officer asked.

"Just one customer," Recker said.

"All right. Watch your head," the officer said, putting his hand on Recker's head as he guided him into the back seat of a police cruiser.

With Recker secure, another squad of officers rushed into the liquor store to check the damage. They immediately ran into Haley before sweeping the rest of the store. As they brought him out to be questioned, he tried his hardest to get Recker off.

"The guy you have over there isn't the one who robbed the place," Haley said.

"Yeah, we know."

"There were four other guys and the guy you got is the one who stopped them. If it wasn't for him, who knows what would've happened?"

"We're not taking him in for this," an officer said. "He's wanted for other things."

"Oh."

"Just sit tight for a few minutes so we can get down your version of everything."

Haley kept his eyes glued on the police cruiser that Recker was sitting inside, hoping that somehow the doors would open, and he'd be released. It wouldn't happen, though. After a few more minutes, a few police cars left the scene, including the one that had Recker. As they started driving through the streets, the officer sitting next to Recker started talking to him.

"I know this don't mean much right now, but I wish I wasn't the one doing this."

"Why's that?" Recker said, looking out the window.

"Honestly? I was hoping you'd never get caught."

Recker stopped his gaze and looked over to the officer, realizing that he had a fan.

"My partner and I are both appreciative of the things you've done in this city. The more filth that you've taken out is less that we have to deal with."

"Well, hopefully I've never made things too tough for you guys," Recker said. "My intention has always been to help you."

"Wish we could just let you go."

"Don't worry about it. It was bound to happen sooner or later."

"Yeah, well, hope you have a good lawyer," the officer said. "Hey, you got any partners or anything that could bail you out?"

"No, I work alone. Besides, I'm pretty sure I'll be one of those guys held without bail."

"Too bad. For what it's worth, I hope you can figure a way out of this thing."

"Appreciate it."

As they drove, the officers seemed to be getting real chummy with their prisoner. It was obvious that they didn't enjoy taking Recker in, though it was kind of a thrill for them to be talking to him. Though the half of the police force that didn't want Recker around all hoped that they'd be the one to capture him, of the half that did appreciate having him around, most wished they could've bought him a beer or two to tell him they enjoyed his work. They were about ten minutes away from the police district they were taking him to. Stopped at a red light, there were no other vehicles behind them. As Recker sat there contemplating his future, he looked toward his left at the intersection and noticed a van speeding around the corner. It took a very wide turn and appeared to be gaining momentum, crossing over the yellow lines.

"Look out!" Recker yelled, trying to warn the officers of the impending danger.

There was nothing they could do to get out of the way. The unmarked van crashed into the front of the police car on the driver's side, spinning it around, facing the opposite direction as it came to a stop. Another car came zooming up the street, tires squealing, and smoke rising, as it halted just in front of the bumper of the police cruiser. Men jumped out of both the car, and the van, hoods over their faces and assault rifles in hand and pointed at the occupants. The two police officers, as well as Recker, were all temporarily stunned by the impact of the collision, though none of them were seriously hurt. The masked men opened the back door to the police cruiser, as the driver started regaining his senses. He reached for his gun, quickly sizing up the situation.

"Don't do it! Don't do it!" one of the hooded men told him, aiming his rifle at the cop's face. "Just sit tight and nobody will get hurt."

Though he wanted to engage their attackers, the officer thought better of it. He knew he couldn't outdraw them, and even if he somehow got the drop on one, the others would see to it that he never lived to see another day. There were at least six men that the officer could see, though there could've been a few more he didn't notice. In truth, there were eight. Four from the van and four from the car. Both of the officers had their guns taken from them and thrown onto the ground. With the door to the driver open, as well as the doors on both sides of the back seat, all the occupants had guns pointed directly at them. Both officers had now regained their senses completely, but were cooperating with the masked men's commands, not that they had much choice in the matter.

"All right, take him and let's go!" One of the men shouted.

The two officers were removed from the car and were ordered to throw their radios on the ground. The masked men stomped on them, smashing them into pieces and rendering them useless. Then, one of the hooded men stuck his rifle into the front seat of the police cruiser, aiming at the center console. He opened up and fired, completely ripping apart their computer and radio equipment as pieces of it flew into the air. Once the shooter was finished making their equipment inoperable, two of the men reached inside the back seat and put a hood on Recker's face, dragging him out of the car. With a man on each side of his arm, pulling him along the ground, they threw him into the opened van rear door. All eight of the hooded men hurried back into their vehicles and sped off, disappearing into the night. As they drove away, the police officers grabbed their guns off the ground, but with their radios and computers destroyed, they had no way of signaling for backup, or of letting anyone know where their attackers had gone.

The van was in the lead with Recker, the other car closely following as they headed to the meeting spot. After a few minutes of driving, they all removed their hoods. The leader of the crew, in the back of the van with Recker, removed his cell phone and called his boss to let him know how everything went.

"It's done, boss," the man said.

"Excellent. Any casualties?"

"Nope. It went off without a hitch."

"Are you being pursued?"

"No, we're good."

"And Mr. Recker?"

"Doesn't seem any worse for the wear. What do you want me to do with him?"

"Bring him to the warehouse as we planned."

"Got it. Should be there in about twenty minutes. Should we take off the hood?"

"Sure. Let's not keep him in suspense any longer. Let him relax a little bit. It's been a trying day for him."

The man did as he was directed and picked Recker up off the floor of the van, sitting him upright. He grabbed a piece of wire and placed it into the keyhole of his handcuffs, twisting it until the cuffs sprung open. He placed Recker against the side wall of the van as he sat back across from him.

"You can take the hood off," the man said.

Curious at who his captors were, and what they

wanted, Recker placed his hand on the top of his head. He grabbed hold of the hood and slowly took it off. He squinted for a moment as his eyes readjusted. It didn't take too long since the hood hadn't been on him for too long. But it only took a few seconds for him to recognize the face of his captor. Recker didn't say a word as he contemplated what was happening. By the look on Recker's face, the other man could see that he was a little shocked.

"Surprised?" the man said.

Recker motioned with his face, indicating that he was. He couldn't figure out how Jimmy Malloy would've known where he was or that he was in trouble.

"Never thought I'd live to see the day that Mike Recker was stunned."

"First time for everything I guess," Recker said.

Malloy sat there, a confident look embedded on his face, content with the feat they just pulled off.

"So are you gonna tell me what this is all about?" Recker said.

"Looks like a rescue to me. Don't tell me you would've been more comfortable sitting inside a jail cell."

"But why? How?"

"You're asking questions that are way above my pay grade," Malloy said.

"Are they? We both know you're Vincent's right hand. You know everything he's planning. I assume this was done with his say so."

"Good assumption."

"How'd you know I was gonna be in that police car? How'd you know what was going down?"

"We got good intel."

"That's not something that was planned in advance. How could you have known so soon?" Recker said.

"Maybe we got an SOS."

"So you're not gonna tell me?"

Malloy shrugged. "Vincent can do that. My job was just to get you."

"So where we heading? We meeting him?"

"Yeah. You've been there before. Same place that you took out the Italian guy... the one that tried to kill you."

"That the new hot spot?" Recker said with a smile.

No matter what the deal was, or the reason behind his escape, at least Recker knew he wasn't getting killed. Well, it was unlikely anyway. It would have been an awful lot of trouble for Vincent to go to if he was just going to bury him later. But considering they had no bad blood, Recker was reasonably sure it wasn't the case. But he also doubted they broke him free just for friendship. Though they were on good terms, breaking him free from the police was a big move. A bold move that Vincent was unlikely to take unless he benefited from it somehow. He figured there must have been another shoe that was going to drop once he spoke to Vincent. He usually had something up his sleeve, or a long-term view on something he was worried about. Maybe he needed Recker for another job. Whatever it was, it wouldn't be long until Recker found out.

The rest of the car ride to the warehouse was quiet, barely a word being spoken by anyone. Recker had a lot of questions, but he knew they were unlikely to be answered by Malloy. He was a good soldier. Loyal. Maybe to a fault. He'd never spill any information that Vincent didn't want leaked out. Not even by accident. He knew his place; he knew his role, and he never overstepped any boundaries. Vincent could never have asked for a better second in command than him.

Once they got to the warehouse, the van parked right in front of the bay doors, followed closely by the car behind them. Malloy was the first to get out, then Recker. Though Recker knew which way to go, he let Malloy lead the way since he wasn't there of his own accord. As they walked up the metal steps, Recker tried to prepare himself for what might've been asked of him in return for the favor of freeing him from the police. He was sure it would be something he wouldn't like. He knew Vincent didn't do it out of the kindness of his heart. He just hoped it wouldn't be something that terrible. They walked across the warehouse floor until they got to the hallway that led to the room they conducted business in several times before. Malloy knocked on the closed door three times then opened it. Vincent was sitting behind the desk, waiting for them, looking relaxed.

"Mike, so nice of you to join us."

"Don't think I really had much choice in the matter."

Vincent smiled, knowing he was technically correct. "True. But you could have taken issue with coming."

"But then I wouldn't have found out what I owe you in return."

"You don't look too worse for wear," Vincent said, looking his visitor's face over closely. "A few bumps and bruises. Should go away in a few days."

Tired of standing, Recker sat down in the chair in front of the desk, across from Vincent.

"Quite a predicament you found yourself in," Vincent said.

"Yeah, sure was."

"So what led to that?"

"Was preventing a robbery," Recker said.

"You stop a robbery and yet you're the one lead away in handcuffs," Vincent said with a smile, seeing humor in it. "The irony is unmistakable."

"I'm glad you see some levity in it."

"Maybe it's time you came over to my side of the fence. After all, if you're going to do good things and help people, and still wind up on the wrong side of the law, what's the point?"

Recker answered almost immediately, not even needing time to think of a reply. "The point is in helping the people that need it. Whatever happens after that is moot. It's not about me."

"Spoken like a true martyr." Vincent laughed. "I'll be sure to say those words over your funeral casket."

Recker also smiled, before getting back to wondering why he was there. "So are you going to clue me in to what favor I need to repay? I know you didn't rescue me for friendship or old time's sake."

"Tomorrow morning."

"Tomorrow morning? For what?"

"For your presence at the meeting. Usual place. Nine o'clock."

"You're gonna keep me guessing all night?" Recker said.

"I'll tell you this; I'm not going to ask you to do anything that would compromise your principles," Vincent said, trying to alleviate his fears without saying too much. "What I need you to do would greatly help me in a situation and would square us in any outstanding matters."

By the seriousness of Vincent's face, Recker could see that whatever it was, it was big. Maybe bigger than anything they've ever had to deal with when doing business together. But it was still worrisome nonetheless that he wouldn't divulge more details.

"Well, you've had a long day," Vincent said. "I just wanted to make sure you were safe and sound. You're free to go if you'd like to go home and relax."

"Well, I, uh, seem to have left my car somewhere. Probably not a good idea for me to be out walking around the streets on a day like this considering there's probably a manhunt going on. Not to mention this is probably the lead story on all the news outlets."

"Of course. Jimmy will take you wherever you'd like to go. Just say the word."

Recker stood up to leave, but quickly stopped himself, realizing that his host hadn't yet answered the biggest question that he had.

"So, uh, about how you found out I was in trouble or where I was?"

"Oh. I received a frantic phone call about your dire situation," Vincent said.

Recker squeezed his eyebrows together, not piecing together who could have possibly called him. "Who else knows the both of us and knew of my problem?"

Vincent grinned, knowing his dangerous friend probably already had the answer to his question if he just thought about it for a few moments. "I believe that is a question you probably already know. Search for the answer within and you shall find it."

Recker looked away for a few seconds, staring at the wall. There was only one answer that came to him, but he couldn't come to grips with it. There was no way that the professor would have called Vincent. There was just no way, he thought. Recker strained his brain to think of another solution, but he kept coming back to Jones. Haley didn't know Vincent. Mia didn't know where Recker was. It had to be Jones. But he still couldn't believe it. He looked back at Vincent, who was nodding at him. Seeing the shocked look on his face, he knew that Recker had come up with the answer.

"Yes, it's true," Vincent said, reading Recker's face.

"He called you?"

"I'm not sure which one of us was more surprised. You just now, or me when I took the call. I guess it just goes to show you the old adage is true."

"Which one is that?"

"About desperation. When a man is desperate enough, there are no lengths he won't go to in order to relieve the tension he feels. When backed into a corner, you'll do whatever it takes to crawl out of it. You, me, your partner, none of us are immune to it."

"I guess that's so."

Recker, still stunned, wasn't sure what else to say or what else he could reveal, without knowing exactly what was said between the two of them in their conversation.

"I know it comes as a surprise to you, but it really shouldn't," Vincent said. "I've always known you've had a partner of some sort. I knew this thing you do couldn't only be the work of one man. There always had to be another, lurking in the background. It's too big of an operation for only one man to take on."

"So what do you plan to do with this little nugget of information you now have?"

Vincent shook his head, not taking offense to any implications that may have been inferred. "Nothing. As I've said before, our relationship has been solid, benefiting the both of us numerous times. That doesn't have to change now. We've both basically left each other to our own devices. We haven't interfered in each other's business. Besides, as I've said, I need your help in a matter. It wouldn't behoove me to jeopardize our relationship over something like this."

Recker nodded, feeling a little better about the revelation, though it was still a little hard to believe. "So what exactly did he tell you about him, or us?"

"Not much actually. As you can imagine, our conversation did not last very long. There were other, more pressing matters that were extremely urgent, as I'm sure you're aware. We only talked of a few specifics before hatching the plan to spring your release."

"Who came up with that?"

"Well, your partner has his skills and I have mine," Vincent said, answering the question without actually confirming anything.

"OK, well, I guess I'll be seeing you in the morning."

"Yes, we will. Can't wait to see the both of you."

Recker had taken two steps, but then stopped dead in his tracks. "The both of us?"

"You and David," Vincent said with a smile.

"David?" Recker said, in shock that his name was actually being used and was now a known quantity.

"Yes. One of the conditions of our agreement was that the two of you would agree to a meeting tomorrow morning to discuss business."

"He agreed to that?"

"He did. You know how I feel about doing business with people. I like to know who I'm dealing with. Coming to agreements and arrangements with strangers is something that I abhor, as you know."

"Tomorrow morning it is, then," Recker said.

Recker followed Malloy out of the warehouse, neither of whom said another word until getting to a car. It was a different one than was used in the police hit-and-run. Those cars would be sitting idly by for a few more weeks until the heat died down. Malloy asked Recker where he was taking him, and even though the cat seemed to be out of the bag now with Jones revealing himself, the Silencer still couldn't let them see the location of their office. Or his home. He'd have to figure out another plan to get back. He quickly thought of Haley, since he was still an unknown. Then he reached down and felt his pocket, remembering that he no longer had his phone. What to do now?

He initially just told Malloy to drive, and after a few minutes, then he'd figure out where he was going. Since he no longer had a phone and couldn't communicate with anyone, he'd either have to walk his way back, or take the risk of being identified and step inside some-where to use a phone. It was just about midnight, and Mia should be getting done soon. He figured the easiest thing to do would be getting dropped off at the hospital. At least some of the people there had already seen his face before, and nobody seemed to recognize him. Or if they did, they never notified the authorities.

Even though it was a hospital, and a public building, it was probably the safest place for him to go at the moment. Though he also knew that would require some explaining to Mia. Not that it really mattered, he thought. He was sure she'd see it plastered on the news, anyway. Malloy got to the hospital in about thirty minutes, a few minutes after midnight. Mia rarely went home on sched-ule, though, usually taking extra time to finish up her duties.

"Figuring on getting checked out?" Malloy asked, thinking a hospital was a strange place to go.

Recker faked a smile. "No, just figured I'd use a phone."

"Probably better places to do it. Might get recognized in there, what with you being a lead news story."

"Some of these people know me. I'll be fine."

"Oh yeah. Now I remember," Malloy said, taking the opportunity to needle him a little. "This is where that girl works, isn't it? You know, the one we rescued from Joe in that building a while back, isn't it?"

"Is it? I don't recall."

"Yeah, yeah, yeah, what was her name? Nancy, Mary... Mia," Malloy said, pretending to forget, though he remembered her name right away. "That was it. Mia."

"Oh, is this where she works?" Recker said, not giving in to the charade.

"You and her ever... you know."

Recker knew full well what he was hinting at, and he wasn't going to play the game with him. He wasn't going to admit that he knew Mia in any capacity, even though he knew it was likely by the way Malloy was talking, that they'd already done their background on her. Recker already knew that Vincent realized there was some connection between him and Mia after the Simmonds situation, but he'd hoped that he eventually let it go. By Malloy bringing it up, it was obvious that they hadn't. Maybe it meant nothing, but maybe it also meant they were still keeping tabs on her. Though it was an important question to consider, with the other things on Recker's plate, it was one that would best be left answered for another day.

"Thanks for the ride," Recker said, closing the car door.

Though he figured police would probably check out hospitals as a precaution, since this one was outside Philadelphia borders, he figured he was safe. Plus, he doubted they would check a pediatric wing for him. As Recker entered the hospital, he noticed a guard near the entrance that he was familiar with, and one that knew Mia.

"Hey, how you doing?" Recker asked. "Did Mia Hendricks happen to leave yet?"

"I don't recall seeing her. Did you check to see if her car was still here?"

"No, I didn't. I'll just go up and check."

With Malloy hanging around, checking for Mia's car was the last thing that Recker wanted to do. It was possible that they already knew which car was hers, but in case they didn't, he wasn't going to be the one that led them to it. Recker went up to the pediatric unit floor, immediately recognizing one of the nurses on the floor as he walked by in the hallway.

"Hey, nice to see you again," Recker said with a smile.

"Hey, you too," the nurse replied. "Come for Mia?"

"Yeah. She still here?"

"I think so. I think she was just about to leave. C'mon, I'll walk back with you and get her."

"Thanks so much."

The nurse led Recker past the locked doors and onto the baby unit, immediately paging for Mia to come to the front desk.

"Hey stranger," another nurse said, noticing Recker as she walked by.

"Hello," Recker replied, a little uncomfortable that so many people there seemed to know him by sight, even if they didn't know who he actually was.

"Hey sweetie, this is a nice surprise," Mia said as she approached him, shocked that he was there. She leaned in to give him a kiss, but quickly removed her lips from his as she noticed his face. "What are those bumps and bruises from?"

Mia put her hands on the side of his face as she inspected it more closely. She was still in her full nursing outfit, so she hadn't clocked out yet.

"You almost done? I'll tell you about it once we leave," Recker said.

"Yeah, give me five more minutes."

"OK. You have your phone on you? I need to call David."

Mia looked at him strangely, knowing something weird was going on. She took it out of her pocket and handed it to him, expecting an explanation as she did. By the look on her face, Recker could see that she was waiting for something.

"I'll tell you when we leave. Finish up," Recker said, dialing Jones' number.

Jones picked up after only one ring, assuming that Mia had seen something on the news and was calling in a panic over it.

"Mia, everything's fine," Jones said, hoping to quiet her fears quickly.

"It's me," Recker said.

"Oh, thank heavens. Are you alright?"

"Yeah, I'm at the hospital right now."

"What are you doing there? Are you hurt?"

"No, but I didn't have my car or my phone. Malloy dropped me off. Figured this was the best spot I could go. Can't exactly be walking the streets right now."

"No, understandable," Jones agreed.

"You heard from Chris? Where's he at now?"

"Chris is fine. He's actually here with me at the office right now. We were just going over the events from tonight."

"That's good. I was worried he might still be stuck with the police," Recker said.

"No, he's fine. They bought his story about being a customer."

"Good."

"So if Malloy already dropped you off, I assume you've already met with Vincent?" Jones asked, worried about how his partner would respond to the news.

"Yeah. He told me we're meeting with him tomorrow morning."

"And?"

"And what?"

"Are you going to blow up at me now or later for revealing myself to him?"

"Neither. You did what you felt you had to do. Nothing I haven't done a thousand times before."

"Yes, but after all the times I reprimanded you over having dealings with him to accomplish whatever task we were working on, and then I basically do the same thing, I figured I have a tongue-lashing coming," Jones said, a little mad at himself for allowing him to be found out.

"It's like I've told you before, sometimes you gotta align yourself with the lesser of two evils to get the job done. I'm sure if there was another option, you would've taken it."

"I know. It's just that there were no other options that I could see," Jones said, still trying to explain his decision making, trying to justify it in his own mind more than Recker's. "Chris was out of the picture, there was nothing Mia or I could do, once you were in the hands of the police, there was little I'd be able to do, outside of getting you a good lawyer."

"Just so you know, I wouldn't have given you up."

"Please, Michael, that was the last thing that ever entered my mind. I have no doubts you would rather spend forty years behind bars than give myself or the operation up. No, my only concern was getting you back, as safely as possible. I just had to hope that Vincent was both willing and able to help. Luckily he was."

"Do you know what this meeting's about tomorrow?" Recker asked, curious if he'd told Jones anything.

"No. I assumed it was a more formal introduction meeting, so he could pick my brain a little."

"I don't think it's that. It seemed more serious than something like that. Like something was really bothering him. I couldn't put my finger on it though."

"Well, whatever the case, we won't have to wait long to figure out what it is."

"I guess you wanna pick me up in the morning? My truck's still at the liquor store. At least I hope it is. Hope they didn't impound it."

"Should still be there. It's not registered in your name. If they run it, it'll come back to a valid citizen."

"You're saying I'm not valid?" Recker said, trying to crack a joke. "I'm hurt."

"You know what I meant."

As Recker hung up, Mia came back over with her jacket on, ready to go. As they walked down the hallways, she started peppering him with questions.

"Do you want to tell me what's going on now? Like where's your phone? Where's your car? Why do you have bruises on your face? I can go on and on."

"Something came up," Recker deadpanned.

"You really think that's gonna satisfy me?"

"No. Satisfies me though."

She gave him a look, indicating that she wasn't

playing games. He tried not to look back at her, knowing that she was burning a hole through him with her stare. But eventually he gave in, as he usually did with her, since she was the one person he had a soft spot for.

"I take it you haven't seen any news reports tonight?"

"No, it's been a busy night. Why? What happened?" Mia asked, the concern in her voice elevating.

Recker then explained to her what went down at the liquor store. He started by saying why it was so important to stop the gang, letting her know how they killed a couple people on their previous job. He figured that would at least somewhat explain why he stayed as long as he did, even at the risk of being caught by the police. But no matter what he said, he knew she wouldn't like him putting himself in so much jeopardy.

"I thought bringing Chris in was supposed to put you in less danger," Mia said as they exited the hospital.

"Well, Chris being there is probably the only reason I'm still here. I might still be locked in a shootout with those guys. He took out two of them," Recker replied, keeping an eye out for Malloy as they walked through the parking lot.

"So now your face is plastered all over the place? Wonderful."

"Mia, nothing's really changed. I've always been wanted by the police. This doesn't change that."

"You know Vincent's gonna ask for something for this. He didn't just do it because he's got a heart of gold."

"I know. We're already scheduled to meet with him tomorrow."

Mia sighed, not liking anything she was hearing.

"Great. Just promise me you won't do something bad in return. Don't just agree to anything he asks just because you feel you owe it to him."

"We'll see what he asks. I promise I won't kill a kid or the mayor or anything," Recker agreed, getting in the driver seat of Mia's car.

As they were driving, Recker could see that she was still steamed. Not that he blamed her. He would've been more surprised if she wasn't. She worried about him. It was part of the deal. But he knew it was better coming from him now instead of her reading or hearing about it later. Satisfied that Malloy wasn't lurking around some-where, Recker exited the parking lot, though he'd still do his usual zigzag pattern on the way home just to make sure. Even if Malloy was still around, Recker would make sure he'd lose him somewhere along the line. The entire drive home, Mia continued to express her concern over Recker's latest situation. Though she knew it wasn't his fault, and he wasn't being careless, she still couldn't help but worry about his well-being. After a few minutes of silence, Recker actually preferred the alternative. Though he didn't like to see her upset, he'd rather have her talking about what was bothering her instead of letting it sit and stew around inside her. Especially when he knew she was still thinking about it.

"I know you're not just gonna let it go at that," Recker said.

"Mike, I told you I don't wanna be one of those nagging girlfriends. I'm not gonna beat you over the head with the same stuff over and over again. You're obviously capable of doing what you do."

"But?"

"But nothing. There's no but. I just know that no matter what I say, it's not going to make a difference. It won't change anything. You're not going to do anything different, right?" she said with a shrug. "So I'm not gonna keep harping on it."

"OK."

Recker thought the issue was closed, but quickly was reminded otherwise. "I can't get the image out of my mind of you in handcuffs in the back of a police car."

"Wasn't that pleasant."

"And being rammed in broad daylight, sitting in a police car."

"It was actually nighttime," he said, trying to bring some levity to their discussion.

"I mean, what's gonna be next?"

"I'll probably find that out tomorrow."

10

Jones had gone to Recker's apartment a little early before heading to the meeting with Vincent. Mia invited him over, so they could all eat breakfast together. Though she liked it when they all shared some time together, part of it was her devious plan to know what the two partners had in mind for their meeting. She wanted to overhear their thoughts and also interject some of her own if the opportunity presented itself. She was a little disappointed that they didn't discuss nearly as much as she thought and hoped they would. Most of it was just general comments and ideas. Nothing specific.

"I must admit, I am a little nervous," Jones said, finishing his eggs.

"Why?" Recker asked. "You've met him before."

"Yes, but those were quite different circumstances. I was pretending to be someone else. Sometimes that's easier than playing yourself."

"I'm pretty sure he knew who you were the moment he met you. Or at least had an inkling."

"I don't doubt that. Still, a little unnerving to be meeting him officially for the first time. What if he asks personal questions?"

"Easy. Don't answer them."

"He won't be offended?"

"He respects people who stand firm in their beliefs," Recker said. "If you're unsure of anything, just look to me, I'll get you through it."

After Mia cleared away the dishes from the table, she sat back down and rejoined their conversation.

"Will you two please promise not to do anything out of the ordinary?" she said. "I know you'll both feel somewhat indebted to him for helping last night, but please don't compromise your principles out of some pride thing or feeling like you have to repay a debt."

"Well, I certainly don't feel the need to do anything of that nature," Jones said, much to Mia's delight. "But I do feel we owe it to him to see what he has to say."

"I agree," Recker added.

"But I won't be pushed into doing something that I will regret, either."

"That's all I ask," Mia said, feeling better about their meeting.

"What you got Chris working on today?" Recker said, wondering about their protege.

"Nothing yet," Jones replied. "I told him to take the morning off and not come into the office until noon. I said if he really wanted to do something productive, just take a drive around town, continue to get to know the city and the streets. He indicated he'd likely do that."

Once 8:15 hit, Recker and Jones finished up what they were doing and left for their rendezvous. Mia worked at noon, and probably wouldn't be home until midnight again, but expected a text or a voicemail letting her know how everything went. She was extremely worried about them agreeing to something they didn't want to do to repay Vincent for helping them out of a tight spot, caving into any pressure that he exuded.

They arrived at the diner a little before nine, but noticed the usual bodyguard standing outside the door, letting them know that Vincent was already waiting inside. Recker placed both of his guns in the glove compartment before getting out of the car. They began walking toward the front door of the restaurant, the guard spotting them as they approached. The guard made a face and tilted his head, putting his hand out toward Recker, both of whom knew the drill.

Recker opened his coat to indicate he was clean. "Didn't bother today."

The guard smiled, then turned his attention toward Jones. "Your turn. Need your iron."

"I beg your pardon," Jones said, insulted that the man thought he was carrying a weapon.

"He doesn't carry," Recker said.

"Still need to check," the guard said, shaking the professor up and down.

Seeing that they were both clean, the guard nodded for them to go inside.

"Well that was a little humiliating," Jones said.

"You get used to it," Recker replied.

As usual, Malloy was there inside the door to greet the pair.

"Nice to see... both of you," he said with a grin.

"I know the way," Recker said, putting his arm out to indicate that he didn't need to be walked to the table.

Jones followed Recker to find Vincent's table, who was sitting in the same spot he always was. Vincent was looking over a menu as his two visitors approached and sat down across from him. The waiter came over as soon as all the men were situated.

"Join me for breakfast?" Vincent said.

"We've already eaten," Recker said.

"Suit yourself. Pancakes for me," he said. "French toast. Orange juice. Bring an orange juice for everyone."

"Yes, sir," the waiter replied.

"David, nice to see you," Vincent said with a smile. "Much easier and more pleasant circumstances than the first time we met. Thank you for upholding your end of the bargain by coming here."

"I can't honestly say that I'm pleased, but a deal is a deal," Jones said.

"So I've always suspected that Mike had a man behind the scenes, getting him the information he needed. I can now safely assume that that's always been you."

"It has."

"So how do you do the things that you do? How do you anticipate where to be? How does that happen?"

"I'm afraid that the secrets of our operation must

remain so. I'm very leery of details getting out," Jones said with a shake of his head.

"I understand."

"Should we get down to the nitty gritty?" Recker said, eschewing the small talk that he hated engaging in. "Though I know getting to meet the brains behind the operation was enticing, I'm sure that's not the only reason you wanted us here."

"Indeed not. As I mentioned to you last night, a very grave situation is encompassing me and my operation right now," Vincent said, a serious tone encompassing his face. "One that I'm at a loss for."

In all the dealings that Recker had with Vincent up to this point, he'd never seen him with a more serious expression. Not with Jeremiah, not with the Italians, and not with any of the cases Recker needed assistance on. This was on another level. After a brief pause, Vincent continued with his problem.

"Approximately two weeks ago, an attempt was made on my life," Vincent said, to the stunned ears of both Recker and Jones.

"Get the guy?" Recker said.

"No. Another attempt was made four days ago. Clearly both attempts failed or else I wouldn't be sitting here. It's obviously of great concern to me."

"When you say attempts were made, what exactly are we talking about? Guns, bombs, what?"

"In both cases it was a gun. The first time was from a rooftop. It narrowly missed me and hit one of my guards standing next to me. I had moved just in time. The second time was from a window across the street. Tried to pick me off just as I had gotten into my car. The bullet shattered one of the windows, but luckily missed any human targets."

"Know who's behind it?"

"We do not. That's one of the things that has me so concerned. Normally, things like this are to be expected from time to time. It wouldn't be the first time. But, I usually know where my enemies are coming from. I can prepare. Anticipate. This is a situation where I cannot do that."

"You have no idea whatsoever?" Jones interjected.

"I've used all the resources at my disposal. Contacts, sources, employees, police, everything has turned up dry. We don't have a single lead to go on."

"And you have no enemies that you're aware of?" Recker said.

"Well, we both know men of my power will attract those who wish to gain what I have. Overthrow me," Vincent said with a shrug. "But whoever it is, is operating completely in the shadows to this point. Nobody seems to have any answers as to their identity."

"Could be remnants of Jeremiah's gang. Or maybe even one of Bellomi's former employees."

"Naturally that's something we thought of as well. It's certainly plausible, and though there are some of both who are still roaming around, we haven't established a connection."

"I would lay odds that it's one of them."

Vincent threw his hands up off the table, neither agreeing nor disagreeing with Recker's statement. He just didn't know at this point.

"So what is it that you would like us to do?" Jones said, assuming there was a proposition coming.

"I've long been an admirer of your operation. And though I don't understand or comprehend much of it, I believe there are things that you can do that I can't."

"And you would like us to look into it for you?"

"I have nowhere else to turn at this point," Vincent said, sounding frustrated. "Though I'll obviously keep looking on my own, I'm not so powerful or oblivious that I can't admit that I could use some help."

"Did you check for any evidence left behind at either scene?" Recker asked.

"We did. There was nothing left at either location, however."

"If we agree to this search, what happens if we locate the person or persons behind it?" Jones said.

"All I ask for is the identity of whoever's behind this. Once that is learned, turn the information over to me and I will take care of the rest."

"And is it expected that we drop everything else we're doing to prioritize this for you?"

"Well, I'm a reasonable man, I know you gentlemen have other things going on. But if you could put a rush on it, I would surely appreciate it."

Jones looked at Recker, wondering what his take on the proposition was. But judging by the non-expressive look on his face, he didn't appear to have one. Recker's motto from the very first day he met Jones was that he wouldn't help criminals. He wouldn't save them, and he wouldn't stand in someone's way if they were in danger. Vincent, however, was a special and unusual case.

Though he was a criminal, there was a certain degree of respect between him and Recker. Plus, Vincent had helped them numerous times before, not the least of which was the previous night.

"Do we have a deal?" Vincent asked, hopeful of their reply.

"We do," Recker said, not bothering to confer with Jones.

"Excellent. Thank you both."

"No need," Jones said, not upset about Recker agreeing to the deal. In fact, he was also leaning on agreeing to it. "After all, you did help us out of a sticky situation last night. I guess we owed you one."

Vincent waved his hand at him. "Ahh, I'm not keeping score. In fact, if you decided not to help in this instance, I'd never bring up what happened last night again."

"Well, we're still very thankful."

Vincent was being truthful when he said he wasn't keeping a tally on how many times they'd helped each other. And while he knew he'd helped Recker out more than the reverse, he never had any plans on using that against him, or as some sort of blackmail. At least not unless it was a situation that was beyond massive in scope. And he couldn't envision that day ever coming. Still, though, he took the opportunity to needle Recker a little.

"Though I do believe I've got the upper hand in favors," Vincent said in jest.

Recker knew his host was just teasing him, but wasn't about to back down to him either. "Maybe so. But I do believe the couple times I helped you were larger in scale than your side with me. I mean, two major mob bosses crippled allowing you to take over, that should have some more weight put behind it."

Vincent laughed, thinking it was probably true. "That's a fair point. Most likely accurate. Quality over quantity, is that how we're putting it?"

Recker didn't reply, instead giving a shrug. Vincent seemed amused by the exchange, while Jones didn't appear to be particularly enthused about the friendly banter.

"So is there anything you need from me to enact what you have to do on your end?" Vincent asked.

"All we need are the exact locations where these incidents took place," Jones told him.

Vincent immediately took out a pen and grabbed a napkin off the table. He wrote down the addresses of the two locations and also scribbled down some rough drawings of the buildings in the area. Once he was finished, he slid it across the table. Jones picked it up and looked at it, and though he recognized the streets, he wasn't overly familiar with it.

"Once we get a handle on what we're dealing with, one of us will contact you in the next few days," Jones said.

"I'll await your call," Vincent said

Though Recker and Jones were quick to leave, wanting to get started on the case right away, Vincent asked them to wait around until he finished breakfast. He wanted to talk about his problem in more detail. Once he finally finished, the three men got up at the same time and walked out of the diner, Malloy closely following. As they exited, the signal was given for Vincent's car to be brought up to the entrance. The driver got out and opened the back door for his boss as Vincent was giving Recker some last words before leaving. Jones was standing beside his partner as they conversed. A white car screeched into the parking lot, and as soon as Recker looked over at it, instantly recognized that it was trouble. As the white car sped toward the diner, Recker pushed Jones down on the ground to make sure he was out of the line of fire. He then quickly grabbed Vincent by his shirt collar and pulled him down behind the car. Just as they were getting down, gunfire started coming from the car. Malloy and the guard at the door returned fire as the car turned around and exited the parking lot.

Before letting either Jones or Vincent up, Recker took a peek over the hood of the car to make sure the danger was gone. Once he saw it was, he grabbed Jones by the back of his arms and helped him to his feet. As he was checking on his friend, Malloy had gotten his boss back to his feet as well.

"You all right?" Recker asked.

"I'm fine. Thank you," Jones said, brushing himself off.

"And you?" Recker said, turning his attention to Vincent.

"I'm good," Vincent said. "Though I'll be much better when you call and tell me you've figured out who's behind this. Do that and I give you my word that you will always have an ally in me, regardless of whether it suits my interests or not."

Recker nodded, appreciating the gesture. "We'll find him."

They then noticed that they did not escape unscathed. The driver of Vincent's vehicle had unfortunately been hit with one of the stray bullets and was on the ground holding his stomach. Recker and Malloy both went over to him to gauge the damage. Vincent stood there, looking on with interest.

"What's his prognosis?" Vincent asked.

"If he gets to a hospital soon, I think he'll live," Recker said.

Malloy looked at his boss, who simply gave him a nod, letting him know to call for an ambulance without even saying a word. Vincent then turned to his other employee, the man who always guarded the door for him.

"You stay with him until he reaches the hospital. Keep me updated on his progress," Vincent said.

"You got it, boss."

Vincent then turned to Recker to give him a few last words. "Thank you for dragging me down. I was a little slow in reacting."

Recker shrugged it off, not needing any thanks. "You'll be hearing from us soon."

"I look forward to it."

As Malloy passed Recker on the way to the car, he gave him a tap on the shoulder. A mutual respect had developed between the two over the years, though neither had trusted the other completely. But now, with this latest development, it seemed to bond them together. Though Vincent had always trusted Recker enough to let him do his own thing, Malloy had always assumed that at one point, he would have to take the Silencer out. It was nothing personal, he just figured he'd step on their toes eventually, and he'd have to be eliminated. Since he was Vincent's right hand, and most trusted soldier, the duty to eliminate Recker would fall upon him. Seeing Recker guard Vincent, and potentially save his life, helped Malloy to see that for the first time, they weren't really on opposite sides.

With their business concluded, Recker and Jones moved along. They got in Recker's truck and went back to the office, immediately starting on Vincent's problem. They were soon joined by Haley, who got in at noon as he was directed.

"Enjoy your driving?" Recker asked.

"Every little bit helps," Haley said. "Know the city better today than I did yesterday. Glad to see you're up and around after last night. Thought I might not see you again."

Recker let out a laugh. "You weren't the only one."

"I'm not ready to go solo yet."

"It should serve as a lesson to all of us how quickly things can go wrong out there," Jones said. "And perhaps should be a lesson that sometimes we need to change tactics."

"Implying that I stayed too long?" Recker asked, assuming he was referring to him.

"I'm not assigning blame, Michael."

"I didn't say you were. But you think I stayed too long?"

"Given the circumstances, yes. Yes, I do."

"Well how else do you think I should've handled it?"

Recker calmly asked. If it was someone other than Jones asking, he might have taken offense to how he handled the situation. But seeing as how it was him, and Recker knew there was no malice in his words, he didn't get upset over being questioned.

Jones threw one of his hands up and shrugged, not sure he had a good answer. "I don't know. What I do know, is that if we overstay our welcome, things like last night will become more commonplace. And we will not always be able to get out of them."

"Should I just leave innocent people in danger to save my own skin?"

"The more ideal scenario might be to not let the situation get to the point it was. Maybe speed things along."

"Maybe we should've taken them out as they were walking through the door," Haley said, offering his own opinion, though he didn't know how welcome it would be.

"Yeah, but, if we didn't take them all out, we would risk having to deal with them again at some point," Recker replied.

"Wouldn't that be preferable than getting led out in handcuffs?" Jones asked.

The three men continued having a spirited discussion, each of them throwing out a few ideas and having them discussed and argued. But there was no bitterness or acrimony in their words. They were only interested in figuring out a better way to handle situations like that in the future, so they wouldn't have to take the chance on someone like Vincent having to bail them out. Because they knew that that would not always be available. It was also something they knew they wouldn't have to deal with often. Recker and Jones had been in business several years without ever getting into a situation like that before, even though there were some close calls at times. Maybe it was just luck that it never happened, or maybe it was because of their careful planning and great execution, but whatever the reason, they had to intensely scrutinize the liquor store event to make sure that it did not happen again.

They discussed the situation from the previous night for a good hour or so, not really coming to a firm conclusion in any capacity. The general feeling after they exhausted all the possibilities was that Recker and Haley probably shouldn't have stayed as long as they did. Whether they took them out quicker, or waited outside, whatever it was, they couldn't engage in a long shootout or get into a hostage situation that would delay their escape. If it was a private residence, or business, maybe they could get away with it. But not in a liquor store in a shopping center that police could get to quickly. Once they had that squared away to everyone's satisfaction, Haley asked how their morning meeting went. Recker and Jones took turns in telling him how everything went down.

"Too bad I wasn't there to help. Maybe I could've got the guy."

"Went too fast," Recker said by way of explanation. "Nothing you would've been able to do. Not unless you were across the lot or something."

As Recker and Haley kept talking about the meeting, along with the attempted murder after it, Jones was already energetically working on leads. He pulled up camera feeds in the area and started combing through them, though he suspected it would be a waste of time and communicated as such to the team. Recker, being with Jones as long as he was, didn't need any more of an explanation. Haley, though, wasn't sure what the issue was.

"Why the negativity?" Haley asked. "Maybe we can get a license plate or something."

Recker smiled, thinking that was the logical conclusion. He let Jones do the explaining though.

"The reason it is likely a waste of time isn't that we won't find anything. There's a decent chance we will," Jones said.

"Then what's the issue? I don't get it."

"Well, Vincent already has men, or women, inside the police department, on his payroll. It stands to reason that he's already had them check nearby cameras."

"Sounds logical." Haley nodded.

"So if that's the case, and assuming it is, it's likely they've already run down a license plate if it was available."

"So it's probably a dead end."

"Presumably. We'll do our due diligence anyway, of course."

"So then what?"

"We dig deeper," Jones said.

"Well how much deeper can you go?"

"We're about to find out."

After letting their conversation finish, Recker had his

own set of questions. Questions that may not be as easy for Jones to answer.

"Why is this the first time we're hearing about this?" Recker asked.

Jones stopped typing and turned to look at his friend, not sure he was getting his meaning. "What do you mean?"

"Well there've been two attempts made at Vincent's life and we've got nothing on it. Haven't heard rumors, nothing came through on the computer, nothing at all. Don't you think that's kind of strange?"

"I suppose so."

"I mean, why didn't we get wind of this?"

"If you're asking whether there's some kind of system glitch on our computers, then the answer would be no," Jones said.

"Sure about that?"

"I am very vigilant in making sure the computers and software are working appropriately and the way they should be."

"So there's no chance of it missing something like this?"

Jones turned away for a second, thinking intently about the question.

"When we started this, I told you I wouldn't help people who had a heavy criminal background," Recker said, remembering their initial conversations. "Did you program it in a way where any leads involving them would get wiped out or nestled away or something?"

"No. They still come in. If they do, and it turns out that the tip is something that involves such a person, I file it away and don't even mention it to you. But it still comes in."

Recker made a grimace, disappointed by the news. He hoped that it would be an easy enough way to check. All Jones would have to do is reset the parameters of the software program and they could work backward. But with Jones dousing Recker's hopes, they'd have to come up with another way.

"The more likely scenario is that we're working with one, possibly two suspects," Jones said, sharing his thoughts.

"And what makes you think that?" Recker said.

"Because I would assume that if it was a larger group, the software would have picked something up. Which leads me to believe that it's one or two people."

"So they don't need to text, call, or email to share their ideas or plans."

"Is there a way that it could be a larger group and the system's just not picking it up?" Haley asked, still not sure of everything the system was capable of catching.

"Of course. But that would mean that they're not using any of the usual code names or phrases that the system flags as a potential concern. And that would be very troubling."

"How many words exactly does the system pick up?"

"There are thousands of words and variations that the system looks for. Any type of threatening word or phrase that you can think of, the system will pick up. And it checks emails, voicemails, text messages."

"Maybe they're working old school," Recker said as a joke. "Maybe they're passing notes to each other in class."

11

W ith having the exact dates and times of the attempted murders of Vincent, it gave Jones a specific starting point to begin his search. His first move was to search through any area cameras, including street and traffic cams, as well as private security cameras that he could hack into. Since the computer program didn't have to comb through weeks and weeks of footage, the results came back quickly. It only took about two hours to get what they needed. Recker and Haley sat down next to Jones as they started looking through the pictures. Jones also began printing them out, so they could look at them more closely.

"You can make out the license plate on that one," Recker said, pointing at one of the pictures on the monitor.

Jones zoomed in on the photo, bringing the license plate number into full view as the letters and numbers grew bigger. He then brought up another screen, typing the number into it, quickly getting back a host of information.

"Well, the license plate number does not belong to that car, for one," Jones said, expecting that to be the case.

"Figures," Recker sighed. "Knew it wouldn't be that easy."

"Stolen?" Haley asked.

"The car in question looks like a Nissan Altima. That plate belongs to a 2013 Hyundai Elantra," Jones replied.

"What next?" Haley said, hoping there was more they could do.

"Now, we see if a camera happened to get a shot of any of the occupants," Jones said.

Jones continued his work, and based upon the locations of the photos they already had of the car, tried to project the path that it traveled. A few more pictures popped up from traffic cameras, but they didn't give them any more information. None of them gave a clear view inside the car. Jones pulled up a few camera feeds from private businesses. After another couple hours of combing through footage, they didn't appear to be any closer to finding their mysterious hit man. Jones was going to keep looking, but Recker and Haley weren't doing much good there. Recker figured they would be better served if they hit the streets to try to find some information.

"Even if we don't get any hits on the cameras that are worth anything, it's still possible we could get something on the email or text software, right?" Haley asked.

Jones stopped typing and turned toward him to answer the question. "It's not likely. Considering they've tried two hits already and we haven't picked up on anything I'd say the chances of us getting something at this point is a remote possibility."

"But still possible," Recker said. "I mean, they don't know we track this stuff. Just because they haven't done it yet, doesn't mean they won't."

"Yes, well, hold on to that thought."

"Well, you keep on with what you're doing, and we'll see what else we can learn."

"How do you propose to do that?" Jones asked, knowing that Vincent most likely already asked everyone that they would.

"Start with the first option as always."

Recker briefly explained to Haley their relationship with Tyrell and the history that they had with him. He then called him on the phone, hoping that he had some nugget of intelligence that he could share with them.

"Tyrell, hoping you can help me with something," Recker said.

"Depends on what you need."

"I don't know if you've heard, but Vincent's had a couple attempts on his life thwarted recently."

"Yeah, I know all about that. Vincent's been trying to pump me for answers. He called me at least five times the last couple weeks to see what I knew."

"Which is what?"

"I'll tell you what I told him," Tyrell said. "I don't know nothin'."

"You haven't heard anything?"

"Haven't heard rumblings, nobody bragging, nobody

threatening to do anything. It's almost like he's getting hit by ghosts."

"Well we know that's not the case. Just off hand, do you know how many men from Jeremiah or Bellomi's former crews are still hanging around?"

"Why? You think one of them might be behind it?"

"It's a thought, isn't it?"

"Yeah. Well most of Bellomi's crew scattered after they got hit. A few stuck around and tried to start brand new again, but they just didn't have the same stones that their boss did. They didn't last too long. Most got picked up by the police, some got killed, but there might only be a handful left. And I don't think they harbor much animosity toward Vincent at this point. I don't think I'm tellin' you anything new, you know all that."

"And Jeremiah's crew?"

"That might be another story. Some of them mo-fo's are still hanging around, and they ain't too pleased about what happened to their boss."

"Stands to reason," Recker said.

"Yeah, well, they ain't too crazy about you either," Tyrell said with a laugh.

"Why? They know I'm the one that did it?"

"They know it was Vincent's doing. He was the one behind it. They don't really care who it was that pulled the final trigger. They know the man that ordered it."

"Then what's the issue with me?"

Tyrell laughed again, thinking some of the beatings he'd taken had taken a toll on his mental capabilities. "You, uh, forget about the two or three places that you took out before Jeremiah got offed?"

Recker thought for only a second, remembering the details vividly. "Oh. Yeah. I do recall something about that."

"Yeah, well, you put about, what, ten or twelve additional bodies in the ground?"

"Something like that," Recker replied, not remembering the final tally.

"And let me tell you, man, everyone knows that was you. Everybody," Tyrell said, his voice rising for emphasis.

"So in your grand opinion, is this the work of Jeremiah's crew, coming back for revenge? Or is it someone new in town looking to take some power for himself?"

"Gotta be one of Jeremiah's boys. At least to me. I got a hard time believing someone new could come in and do this without leaving some type of trace, know what I mean?"

"Yeah, that's what I figured too."

"You mean you and the prof can't figure this out yet? He can't work his magic on the laptop?" Tyrell sarcastically asked.

"Not so far."

"Wow. Never thought I'd see the day when you two were completely stumped like this."

"It's happened before."

"Oh, by the way, there was something else I wanted to talk to you about."

"Such as?"

"You know I opened that 529 account for my brother, Darnell, like you told me to."

"Good move."

"Yeah, well, I put about two thousand in there to start it out with."

"Strong start."

"That's the crazy part. I put that in there about six months ago, right?"

"Yeah."

"Well, I just checked yesterday and guess what? You know how much is in there?"

"Haven't the foggiest idea," Recker said, playing dumb.

"There was fifty thousand dollars in there, man. Fifty thousand. Five-O," Tyrell said, almost in disbelief of the amount.

"Wow. Looks like you made a good investment."

"Yeah, I don't think that was it."

"Hmm. Guess you got one of those mysterious bene-factors," Recker said. "They seem generous. Hope you don't do anything to piss them off."

"Yeah, well, between you, me, and the wall I'm staring at right now, we all know who that person is."

"Now, now, Tyrell, don't snap to quick judgments that may not be correct."

"Are you gonna try to tell me it wasn't you?"

"Well, it may or may not be just me... or other people."

"Prof too?"

"I'll have to plead the fifth on the rest of this conversa-tion," Recker said, not wanting to admit to his good deed.

"I hear ya on that. But seriously, I just wanted to tell you and the prof thanks," Tyrell said, starting to choke up on his words. Not being used to people offering such generous gifts, he usually had trouble articulating how thankful he was when it happened. But he didn't have to. Recker knew. So did Jones. And they knew the money was going to good use in Darnell's education. There was a kid with a good head on his shoulders. Recker and Jones periodically checked in on Darnell from a distance, making sure his grades were still good, making sure he was staying out of trouble, and just touching base with Tyrell about him. For Recker and Jones, money was not an issue. They had more than they knew what to do with and they certainly didn't mind spreading it around, especially when they were invested in the cause.

"Now that we're done with that, any ideas on which of Jeremiah's men might be behind this? A name? Anything?"

Tyrell sighed, trying desperately to think of a name. Unfortunately, he couldn't come up with one. None of Jeremiah's men, in his opinion, could've conducted such a stealthy operation on their own. Maybe with Jeremiah's guidance they could have, but not by themselves, not without him steering their direction. "No, I can't think of anyone offhand."

"And you haven't heard of a new player in town?"

"No."

"Well, I would think that if it was someone new, they would've announced their presence by now," Recker said.

"Maybe they figured Vincent's body would do the announcing for them."

"Yeah, maybe."

"I'll do you a solid though and keep my ear to the

ground for you," Tyrell said. "If I pick up on anything I'll let you know."

"Appreciate it."

As Recker was talking, Jones kept working away, though he kept one ear somewhat listening to the conversation in the background.

"Judging by your side of it, I take it Tyrell wasn't much help," Jones said.

"No. Vincent already asked him anyway."

"Well we kind of figured that, didn't we? After all, Vincent already has him on the payroll, even if it's on a part time, or as needed basis. And considering Tyrell's closeness to Jeremiah as well, not to mention how connected he is on the streets, it's no surprise that he would have already reached out to him."

"The software that picks out these phrases, there's an area radius that it reaches, right?" Haley asked. "I mean, it's not picking up incidents in California or anything, right?"

"Yes, why?" Jones said.

"What if we expand the radius? Is it possible to do a search of the rest of the country and see if it can spot phrases that would indicate an outside person?"

Jones looked perplexed for a few seconds, not exactly sure what Haley was asking. After a little more thought, he got the gist of it. "If you're suggesting that I extend the parameters to include other parts of the country to see if we can find someone, say in San Jose, who's come into town for the purpose of eliminating Vincent, then yes, that is something I can do."

"How long would something like that take?"

Jones bulged his eyes out and blew his lips together, signaling it would be a tall task. "Something of that magnitude would take quite a while. Weeks at the earliest. But that is at a breakneck speed with everything falling our way. I suspect that it would probably take months to go through that amount of information. You're talking about the entire country instead of one city and millions upon millions of data that needs to be broken down. When I was at the NSA, the process could be streamlined much more quickly. But that's with dozens of analysts working on it nonstop. Not one person."

"What if you whittled it down?" Recker asked, thinking they could cut the process down. "Make it faster."

"In what way?"

"Only include phrases that would indicate Philadelphia. Airport, landmarks, the city itself, things like that."

"Well that would certainly speed things up a bit, but you're also taking the risk that they actually mentioned one of the things you're talking about. There's no guarantee they talked in any of those specifics."

"How about in subsequent messages? What if they mention killing in a text, then mention the airport in another?"

"Mike, that all can be done, and the system will pick those things up. But again, it takes time. The system analyzes millions of bits of data. Once it flags something, then it will have to be checked against whether the same user is a threat, whether that user actually has evil intentions, whether that user has said similar things, who they're talking to, and which means of communication they're using. It all can be done. But it will take time. Time that I'm not sure Vincent has. Or has the patience for."

"So what you're basically telling me is that we need to find someone out there on the street who knows what's going on," Recker said.

"It certainly would be helpful."

Recker wasn't really satisfied with the answer, but he accepted it for what it was. Jones would keep doing what he did best, but it was likely he wouldn't have an answer any time soon. And that was assuming that the shooter was from out of town, which was no guarantee. Jones could have been wasting his time in even looking in that direction. Recker took a step back and started thinking of other alternatives. He wasn't going to just sit there and wait for the system to come up with a match. Him and Haley needed to hit the street and see what they could shake loose. Somebody had to know something. It was just finding the person that did. After a few minutes of deep thinking, he thought he might have come up with something. At least something to start with.

"Hmm," Recker said, looking at Haley.

"What?" Haley replied, thinking he might have done something.

Recker shook his head. "Nothing. Just thinking."

"Would you like to share with the rest of us?" Jones asked, hurriedly typing away at his keyboard.

"Do we still have the list somewhere that Tyrell gave us a while back of Jeremiah's hot spots?"

The question made Jones stop typing as he turned

and looked at his partner, unsure of his exact plans, though getting a general idea. "Why?"

"We need information. Maybe someone there has it. Simple as that."

"Assuming that one of Jeremiah's former soldiers is behind this. And assuming that those locations are still in business."

Recker shrugged. "Not really making any assumptions. Just a place to begin."

"But we don't know they're actually involved."

"Don't know they're not either. We know that some of Jeremiah's men are still out there. That's a fact. And we know that they're dangerous. Not on Jeremiah's level, but anyone who carries a gun has to be respected in some form."

"OK. I agree with all that so far."

"So it stands to reason that maybe they know what's going on. If they're behind it, maybe one of them let's something slip. Or, maybe they'll steer us in the right direction," Recker said.

"Considering what you've done to several of their locations already, I believe the only place they'll steer you is over a bridge. A very high one."

"With your history, what makes you think they would tell you anything?"

"Probably not deliberately. But when the emotions start to get high, things sometimes come out that were not intended."

Jones looked at Recker for a few moments without responding, not liking his choice of words. It sounded to him like his partner was considering provoking a conflict in order to get a calculated response.

"You're not thinking about hitting one of these spots with guns blazing, are you?"

"No, not with guns blazing," Recker said with a laugh. "Maybe just on high alert though."

"Mike, we have other things going on right now. Getting into a war with the remnants of Jeremiah's gang doesn't exactly sound like the prudent thing to do at the moment."

"I don't have any intention of starting a war. Just want some information. But usually people whose emotions are running high or angry have a tendency to talk without thinking. That's what we need right now. People who say something without realizing what they're talking about."

"Again, you think they're going to say something useful to you?"

"Well, I have a way of drawing things out of people."

"Yes, usually their lifeline."

"No, well, yeah, but not in this case. If I can get them angry, they might say a thing or two we can use to our advantage."

"And just how do you plan on doing that?" Jones asked, still not on board with the idea.

"Just by showing up. People have a tendency to talk when I'm around. Usually out of fear, sometimes out of anger."

"I think you have officially lost your mind."

"Maybe. But if I show up at their door, they're gonna

know something's up. If they don't wanna join their boss, they'll give me something."

"A gun in the ribs most likely."

"Don't be such a worrywart. It'll work. Usually when people see me, they either start to get worried or mad. Either should work for this."

12

After only a few minutes of searching, Jones found the list of Jeremiah's meeting spots in one of the desk drawers. He handed the paper over to Recker, who looked it over for a few moments.

"Where do you plan to start first?" Jones said.

"At the top," Recker replied. He then turned toward Haley to see if the newest member of the team wanted to join him in the festivities. "Feel like having some fun?"

"It'd be my pleasure," Haley said with a smile.

"Just remember to check in," Jones said, hoping that they wouldn't run into too much trouble.

"Would it be faster and easier if we split up? Each take a building?"

"Faster maybe," Jones replied. "Not easier. If you two are going to do this, I prefer you stick together. These aren't run-of-the-mill criminals we're dealing with. Even without Jeremiah's leadership, they're still dangerous. And likely heavily armed."

"David's right," Recker said.

"But after we hit the first couple, they're going to know we're coming," Haley said. "And they'll either scatter or they'll bunker down and be waiting for us. Might walk into something."

"Possible. But I'd rather hit them hard in the beginning and take our chances later. Strength in numbers and all that."

Haley nodded, OK with the plan no matter which direction they went. "Works for me."

Haley was an easy-going type of guy. He wasn't the kind of person who vigorously argued over much. He didn't have a problem voicing his opinion, or offering a different option, but once a decision on something was made, he usually went along with it without a problem. Unless he was extremely opposed to something, for the most part he just fell in line, and he did so gladly.

Recker and his partner left the office right away, hopeful that they would find some useful information somewhere along the way. In Recker's previous path of destruction when he was looking for Jeremiah, he'd only taken out three of his locations. There were still another seven on the list. Though it was possible that they no longer were doing business in any of them, Recker had a hunch that the places were still in operation. They knew some of Jeremiah's men were still kicking around so it seemed likely that they were staying in the locations that they knew so well. Plus, since Recker wasn't there the first time around, they had no reason to believe the addresses had been compromised.

Since they were going to the same place, Recker and Haley drove together. Recker thought about going separately, just in case they needed to split up for anything, or if they had to track down different leads if they learned anything after they hit Jeremiah's house, but he figured it was better if they just stayed together for the moment. As they were driving to the first location, an address in the western part of the city, Haley wondered what they were walking into. He wasn't around for their previous dealings with Jeremiah and his crew and was curious about the type of people they were dealing with.

"So what are we likely walking into?"

"What do you mean?" Recker said.

"Well I wasn't here for all the fun you had with these guys before. I've only heard you and David talking about them. I haven't met any of them yet. What kind of people are they?"

"Dangerous," Recker said bluntly.

"I kind of figured that."

"They're of the talk less and shoot more variety."

"Oh good," Haley said, rolling his eyes.

"If we actually see someone and get to talk to them, keep your guard up at all times. Don't get complacent, even for a second. Don't trust any of them."

"Good to know. How many you figure are there?"

"Hard to say. Under Jeremiah, there seemed to be a different crew stationed at each location. I think usually between four and six people were there doing their thing," Recker said, remembering from his previous encounters. "Who knows if that's still accurate with Jeremiah gone."

"You think they have a new leader or you think they're all just scattered about, doing their own thing?"

Recker thought about it for a minute, not sure he had a good answer. "I dunno. Could be either I suppose. I guess it depends on whether the next highest in command had enough respect to get everyone else in line. Haven't heard much out of the gang since Jeremiah's death, and Vincent hasn't seemed very concerned with them, so maybe they have no leadership. I guess we'll find out soon enough."

Ten minutes away from their target location, Jones texted them some of the information he pulled up on the address. It was a row home in a rougher neighborhood, the owner of which he could not establish. Though there was a name of an owner listed, he couldn't find any additional information on the man. He assumed it was a fake identity. Jones tried to find out if the house was currently in use for anything, though he couldn't find anything that definitively proved whether it was or wasn't. They just couldn't tell if they were walking into anything or not. It could be a hot zone, or it could be completely abandoned.

As per his usual custom of not directly parking in front of where he was going, Recker parked down the street. Before getting out of the car, he and his partner put the com devices in their ears. In most cases, Recker would've preferred that they split up, with him taking the front while Haley covered the rear of the building. But the house was in the middle of a block with another house directly in back of it. Considering the neighborhood that they were in, Recker didn't want to take the chance of Haley getting in trouble. Especially if he was hopping fences, walking through other people's properties, and hanging out in their backyards. He didn't want him taking a stray bullet from a gun-happy homeowner who mistook him as an unscrupulous character. As they walked down the street, they kept their eyes peeled at their surroundings, while also periodically looking at the house to detect any movement coming in or around it. As they got closer, they could see most of the windows were boarded up with pieces of plywood. There was only one window on each of the second and third floors that were open.

There was a metal fence and gate at the end of the sidewalk that led up to the house. Recker stood on the opposite side of it for about thirty seconds, just staring at the house as he analyzed it before they approached. Sometimes before he got into a situation, he would get a feel for it first, like he would get a sense that something bad was inside. There'd be a feeling of danger. He wasn't getting that in this instance. It was just like a blank space. He wasn't getting any vibes at all. Haley hadn't been involved in this operation long enough to really get that same sense of things. Even though he was an experienced operator in the CIA, it was still a new type of game for him.

"What do you think?" Haley said, not taking his eyes off the house.

"I don't know. I'm not getting anything right now."

"What do you wanna do?"

Recker made an agonizing face as he contemplated. "Move forward I guess."

Recker unlocked the gate from its latch as the two of them entered the property. Neither had their gun out yet, as they didn't want to give the impression that they were there for a battle if someone was watching. They both had their hands on the grip of their gun, though, just in case they had to react quickly. Their eyes were glued to the front door of the house, as well as the two opened windows, making sure that they weren't in the crosshairs of a shooter. They didn't notice a thing. Everything seemed quiet. But Recker also knew that sometimes meant the worst was about to happen.

As they stepped onto the porch, Recker and Haley looked at each other, both waiting for the other shoe to drop. They stopped and listened, hoping to hear a commotion on the inside, though all they heard was silence. Recker motioned for Haley to stand on the other side of the door. He was about to knock and didn't want Haley catching a gut-full of lead if the people on the other side of the door decided to open fire instead of answering. Considering nobody had come out to greet them yet, it was a distinct possibility. After Haley was in place, he finally removed his gun and readied himself to use it. Recker then stood on the other side of the door and huffed before knocking. He knocked loudly and made sure he was out of the line of fire as he awaited a response. A few seconds went by and Recker tried again. Still nothing. As Recker looked at Haley, he raised his eyebrows and shrugged, assuming that nobody was home. Trying to remain as silent as possible, Haley gave some hand signals, wondering if they should leave the premises. Recker returned the signals with a few of his own, pointing at the door, indicating that they should breach it. He then got out his weapon, which was a language that they all understood. Haley nodded in approval, waiting for Recker to take the next step.

Recker took a few steps back, then raised his leg and took a kick at the door. His first try at breaking it open was unsuccessful. He now hoped that the place was empty, because if it wasn't, anybody on the inside who didn't know he was there... well, they did now that they heard the door being kicked in. On his second try, Recker succeeded in kicking the door open. Recker, followed closely by Haley, rushed through the front door with their guns drawn, ready to fire. Silence still filled the air.

Recker motioned to Haley to check the upstairs while he checked the first floor. Though they suspected they were alone, they still kept alert in case they were being set up. Recker swept through the first floor, not finding anyone or anything out of the ordinary. After a few minutes, Haley came stomping down the stairs, also coming up empty. They met back up in the living room, Haley wondering what their next step was. Recker was casually walking around, trying to find anything that would be of interest to them. A piece of paper, a picture, anything at all.

"What are you looking for?" Haley asked.

"I dunno. Anything that would give us more than we got now."

The entire home was virtually empty. There were a few remaining pieces of furniture, but it didn't appear that anyone had been there for some time. The refrigerator was empty; the cupboards were bare, there were no clothes in any closets, nothing that appeared anyone was living there.

"Doesn't seem like anyone's been here for a while," Haley said.

"Yeah. I don't even think it's been used for business purposes either."

"What makes you think so?"

"A lot of dust."

"Maybe they forgot to bring the maid in."

"I don't see a table, chairs, nothing that would indicate somebody's been here," Recker said. "Even if you're just stopping here once in a while for business, you still gotta sit I would think. Unless they're doing it Indian style."

"What now? Next stop on the list?"

"Yeah. We'll send David a message and let him know we came up empty here."

They did as Recker suggested and sent Jones a text to let him know what they found on the first stop of their tour. The next stop was another house. Jones had already run the information on it, anticipating that the first stop was going to return no tangible results. Much like the previous house, Jones couldn't pull up the legit owner of the house, figuring it was also a fictitious name. When Recker and Haley got there, it proved to be a similar situation to the one they just left. Right down to the dust. It didn't look like anybody had been at the second location for some time either.

"What now?" Haley asked, a little frustrated at coming up with nothing at the first two locations.

"We keep moving on."

Recker was determined to check out every single address on the list. There was a good possibility they'd all wind up being empty, but he still had to look and make sure. If there was even one single thing that they could find at any of these locations, it'd be a worthwhile effort. He wasn't discouraged yet or giving up hope that they'd find anything. Just like the first time, they called Jones to let him know their findings. He wasn't as convinced that moving forward with the list was as good of an idea.

"Mike, you know what they say about insanity," Jones said.

"That's only if you keep doing the same thing over and over again and expecting a different result."

"And what do you think you're doing?"

"I'm not expecting anything," Recker said. "We only have three more spots on the list. You never know what might turn up. If we stop now, how do you know we won't miss something? Might as well finish it off. Besides, what else we got right now?"

"Very well."

They finished their talk and Jones texted the information he had on the next location. Once they arrived, it was eerily similar to the last two stops. Quiet as could be. No signs of life. They moved on to the next address, not expecting anything different than they'd found up to that point. They were not surprised or disappointed at finding nothing once again. They moved on to the last spot on the list, assuming they would again find an empty house. The last location was a little different than the others though. Like the others, it was currently unoccupied. The biggest difference was that instead of a residential address, it was a business. It used to be a dry-cleaning business that closed up shop several years earlier. Recker and Haley sat in their car and watched the front of the store for half an hour, not seeing anyone go in or out.

"Figure it's vacant like the others?" Haley said.

"Well, chances are good. But maybe we'll get lucky."

"How soon you wanna hit it?"

Recker looked at the time. "Let's give it another thirty minutes."

Thirty minutes went by, still not a sign of life anywhere. Several people walked along the street, all of whom passed right by the store. They didn't think waiting any longer would make a difference, so the two men got out of the car.

"There's gotta be a back door," Recker said.

"I'm on it. I'll let you know when I'm in position," Haley replied.

Recker started walking on the street, browsing through some of the front windows of the stores that were open, waiting for a sign from Haley that he was ready. After a few minutes, he got it. The back alley of the stores was not especially big, just large enough to get a delivery truck in if needed. Haley was squatting next to a large, green trash dump as he watched the dry-cleaning business. He kept looking up and down the street to make sure there was nobody else back there who saw him. The back door to the business was a solid-colored door, so he couldn't look through it to see inside.

"Mike, I'm in position."

"Roger that. I'm about to enter through the front."

Haley started to move from his position but noticed a car zooming in from the far right end of the alley. He quickly scurried back to his position behind the trash container as he watched the car stop right in front of him. Four men exited the car and walked over to the back door of the dry-cleaning shop.

"Mike, hold up," Haley said, not wanting his partner to walk into something.

"What's up?"

"A car just pulled up back here. We got four men entering the store from the back."

Haley watched the group intently as they milled around the door, waiting for it to open. He noticed one of the men pull out a gun and hold it in his hand before putting it away again.

"They're armed," Haley said quietly.

"You gonna be able to get in back there?" Recker said.

"Uh, not sure. I don't think so."

"Meet back at the car."

As soon as the men had disappeared into the store, Haley moved from his position and went back to Recker's SUV. Recker lifted up the trunk door and started looking through some of the gadgets he had. Haley also started rummaging through some of the weapons his partner had come up with over the years. He pulled over a black bag and unzipped it, going through the contents. He pulled out something, almost in awe.

"Is this what I think it is?"

"Block of C4," Recker said. "Ever use it before?"

"Yeah."

Recker grabbed two assault rifles, throwing one over each shoulder as they got ready. Haley put down the explosives and did the same.

"How you figure on making entry?" Haley asked. "The

only way I'm getting through that back door is if I blow it open."

Recker wasn't averse to the idea, but he was wary about an explosion. He only had a small amount, basically enough to blow open a fortified door, and it wasn't enough to damage anything in the surrounding area as long as nobody was within fifty feet of the explosion. But it would make a noise and there would be smoke. Considering they'd have to likely fight their way afterward, he didn't want to take the chance of police coming soon after that. He'd already had one run-in recently, and after having a close shave, didn't want to do it again so soon.

"Let's hold off on that for now," Recker said. "I don't wanna bring too much attention. Plus, we're still gonna have to look around after we're done in there. After the explosion, who knows how much time we'd get until the cops show?"

"So what's the plan?"

"Knock on the door and kill whoever gets in our way."

"Whatever happened to just talking?"

"OK. Knock first. If they look like they wanna talk, fine. If not, then shoot."

After Haley made sure his weapons were ready to go, he ran back to his former spot behind the trash container. The car was still parked in back of the building. Once he gave Recker the sign he was ready, both men approached their respective doors. Recker tapped on the glass door in front, while Haley knocked on the rear door with the muzzle of his rifle. Recker kept trying several times but got no response. Haley's endeavors were a little more successful. After only a couple of knocks, the back door opened just a hair. Haley made sure he was to the side of the door, so they couldn't look out and see who or where he was.

"What you want?" the man asked, seeming uneasy about the stranger.

Before Haley had a chance to answer, the man noticed the assault rifles on his shoulder and immediately felt threatened and tried to close the door. Haley rushed over to him, blocking the door closing with his shoulder. The man that answered ran back inside the building, screaming all the way.

"Cops!" the man shouted.

"Mike, they're on the run," Haley said.

Recker knew at that point that talking was unlikely and had to get inside quickly to help his partner. Though Haley saw four men enter, there was no telling how many were already in there. They knew there was at least one, since the other four men were let into the building, but they had no way of knowing how many more. They had to be ready for anything. Recker used his gun to break the glass and stepped inside the store, pieces of glass crunching underneath his footsteps. He was somewhat surprised that he wasn't met with a hail of bullets. A second later, he heard the sounds of what seemed to be some chaotic yelling coming from the back of the store.

"I'm in, Chris," Recker said.

As soon as the words left his lips, gunfire ripped through the air. "I'm engaged," Haley said, under fire.

"Coming your way."

As he waited for his reinforcement, Haley returned

fire, hitting two of the men that he recognized from getting out of the car. Recker raced through the building to get to where the action was. He still had to remain cognizant of any surprises coming his way as he did, though. Although the battle was in the back, he did pass a couple of doors that he had to clear. He couldn't take the chance of someone sneaking up on him from behind after passing them. The first door was closed, but he kicked it open and entered. It was a small room but appeared to be an office as there was a desk inside. There was a man sitting behind it who was feverishly trying to put stuff away after hearing the chaos coming from the back. He was the leader of the group, and since they all assumed it was cops hitting them, was trying to get rid of any incriminating evidence. As soon as Recker kicked the door open, the man stood up, surprised they got to him so quickly and before he finished what he was doing. Recker didn't wait and take the chance of the man drawing a gun on him and immediately opened fire, hitting him three times in the chest. Since he could tell there was no one else in the room, he left to clear the next one.

Recker exited the office and went a few feet down the hall to the next room. He kicked it open and immediately saw a couple guns pointing right at his face. Recker instantly dropped to his knees as the bullets flew over his head. From his new position on the ground, Recker returned fire, hitting both of his targets, causing them to fall over from the bullets that were now permanently a part of their bodies. He quickly got back to his feet and rushed inside the room, pointing his gun around in anticipation of using it again, though there were no more hostiles there. He went back to the two men he just put down to check on their status. They were both dead.

At that point, Haley wasn't too far removed from where he first entered the building. They had him pinned down to where he really couldn't move, though they couldn't get past him to get out of the building either. After a few more rounds of exchanging fire, Haley finally finished off the remaining two members of the group.

As Recker came out of the office and walked down the hallway, he noticed that the gunfire had stopped. Until he heard and saw Haley, though, he wasn't assuming that they were in the clear yet. With his gun in the air, he cautiously continued walking toward the back of the building. Once he got to the end of the hall, he noticed several bodies lying on the floor, blood pouring out of them.

"Chris?"

"Yo," Haley said, putting his rifles back on his shoulder as he walked over to him.

Recker looked him over, making sure he had no newfound holes in him. "You good?"

"A lot better than them, that's for sure."

"I think we got them all. I got three back there."

"I got five here. They yelled police when I got in, they thought we were cops. Well, there's no doubt they were up to no good. Were they the ones we were looking for, though?"

"They were Jeremiah's men all right. Now we just have to see if there's a connection to Vincent. There was an office back there that one of them was doing something in," Recker said. "Lot of papers and things. Looked like he was trying to pack up and move in a hurry. Maybe there's something there we could use."

"We're gonna have to move quick, though," Haley said, remembering their last outing together at the liquor store. "People are surely gonna report that gunfire. Police will be here soon enough."

"We'll just grab what's there and go. We'll look through it and sort it out later."

They went back to the office where Recker shot his first man and started rummaging through the papers on the desk. Most were already in folders or binders, making it a little easier to transport. Haley noticed a cardboard box in the corner of the room on the floor and picked it up. He brought it over to the desk and the two of them dumped every piece of paper they saw inside. After being satisfied they had everything, Recker carried the box through the back of the store. Haley led the way with his gun drawn, making sure everything was still clear for them. Seeing that the back alley was still clear, they went back to Recker's car and drove away, just as they heard police sirens in the background coming closer.

13

Before Recker and Haley made it back to the office, they let Jones know of the latest happenings. He was afraid of a shootout happening, though he wasn't surprised. But, at least they made it back. That was his main focus.

"Nice to see you made it back without handcuffs," Jones said.

"Get pinched one time in five years and you never hear the end of it," Recker said to Haley.

Recker put the box of papers down on the desk and, along with Haley, started to remove the contents. Jones swiveled his chair over and started digging into it immediately.

"We can handle going through this stuff if you got other things to do," Recker said.

"Well, the computer is already starting to go through the search guidelines, so I have some time to fill until we get any hits back. Do you think we will actually find anything in this mess?"

"Who knows? Can't hurt."

"Even if we don't find anything related to the Vincent case, we might find out something else," Haley said. "Maybe a different crime we can prevent."

Recker looked at him and nodded, thinking he got the idea. The new guy was fitting in nicely. He was not only an expert shot, and good in sticky situations, but he seemed to understand the long-range view of their operation.

There was a lot of information that they had to go through. There were at least a dozen binders and folders that were full of papers. Each one had a specific purpose that was useful to Jeremiah's operation. Notes, bills of sale, information on hundreds of people, assets, just about anything someone could think of, it was there. Almost immediately, they recognized that it was still Jeremiah's crew they were dealing with.

"I never realized just how in depth and organized Jeremiah's operation was," Jones said, shuffling papers around, somewhat impressed by the depths of the late leader's organization.

"Yeah, he really did keep tabs on just about everything." Recker nodded absentmindedly.

"What exactly are we looking for?" Haley asked.

"Anything that can be useful in any way," Jones said. "Either something that indicates a future problem that we need to stop, or something that indicates they're the ones behind Vincent's issues."

"You'll know it when you see it," Recker said.

The three men sat at the desk for a couple hours, reading every single piece of paper in detail, sometimes two or three times just to make sure they didn't miss anything. Each of them had a separate stack. When they were done with one paper, they put it in a pile for someone else to go through later. Just when they were beginning to think it was a useless endeavor, something caught their interest.

"Wait a minute," Recker said. "Here's something."

"What is it?" Jones asked.

Recker held up the paper in the air, reading parts of it. "Looks like a payroll sheet."

"How many names on it?" Haley asked.

Recker quickly counted the names. "Twenty."

"Well, fourteen now probably. I think you can cross six of those off."

"I can pull up information and photos of these twenty and see if any of them are the ones you just disposed of," Jones said.

While Jones started his task, Recker and Haley continued on with their reading. Thirty minutes later, they stopped once more, again finding something of interest.

"This is kind of weird," Haley said.

"Whatcha got?" Recker said, putting his paper down and looking at what his partner had.

"Looks like some kind of memo or email that they printed out," he said, reading it aloud.

"If you want me to do this job, you're gonna have to pony up a lot more. A million isn't enough."

"Any name on that?" Recker asked.

"No, lists the to and from emails though."

"Let me have that," Jones said, putting his hand out.

"I'll see if I can cross reference the names from the email addresses."

Haley continued looking through a few more papers, but Recker sat still, not moving. He stared at the wall as he contemplated what the memo meant. A million dollars for a job. It had to be something big. Taking out the leader of a criminal organization would certainly qualify.

"That's gotta be it," Recker said, breaking free of his trance.

"What?" Haley asked.

"The needle we're looking for. A million dollars. That's gotta be for taking out Vincent."

"That's a big leap to make, Mike," Jones said. "It certainly is possible, but we need more solid evidence to be able to link the two together."

"You need evidence. I just need a hunch. A gut feeling."

"You could be right. I'm just saying it's a bit premature to say so at the moment."

"Would be nice to be able to get into their bank account records too. Seeing the flow of that million dollars would lead to a few answers."

"Assuming that it's already been paid. And assuming that it's going the way you think it is."

"What do you mean?"

"Well did you ever think that maybe it's someone offering Jeremiah's crew a million dollars to do something? Something completely unrelated to Vincent?"

"Of course it did," Recker said. "I just chose to dismiss it."

Jones rolled his eyes. "Oh. Sounds logical."

Recker went over to Jones' computer and bumped him off. "Let's make this go quicker. Me and Chris will work on getting these jokers names and photos. You get the names associated with those emails. And if you could get bank information, that would be real helpful too."

"If I could get bank information he says. Just like that," Jones whispered, mocking him. "As if it were that easy."

The three men then got to work on their respective assignments, none of which proved to be too difficult. Recker and Haley had the names and photos of all twenty men they were looking for within an hour. They got the pictures from DMV records, social media accounts, as well as police mug shots. Up to that point, they didn't look at the photos too closely, wanting to wait until they were completely finished before they started matching them up. Once they crossed the last name off the list, Recker and Haley started looking at the pictures more intently. They didn't recognize the first few pictures, but then, it started to look a little familiar.

"He was one of them," Haley said, pointing at the picture.

The next picture was another one from the battle. When they were done looking at all twenty photos, they had successfully matched all six of the men from the dry-cleaning store to the names on the payroll list. They let Jones know of their findings.

"Well, all six from the store were on the list," Recker said. "They're down to fourteen."

"Assuming that's everyone that's left in their organization," Jones replied, not sounding impressed. "It's a broad assumption to think that's it. There could still be more."

"Could be. But at least we've identified some of them."

After a little while, Jones started to unearth some interesting information on his end. He got names and addresses from both emails. He grabbed a piece of paper and started writing everything down that was on the screen. He then alerted his partners of his findings.

"I've got it," Jones said.

"What's the deal?" Recker said, him and Haley moving over.

"The email was sent from an address down in Atlanta. The receiving party was here in Philadelphia. I've already cross-referenced the name, and it was on the list that we discovered."

Recker looked at the paper then went back to grab the list of twenty names that he and Haley had just tracked down. The name was one of the ones that they crossed off after perishing in the battle at the dry-cleaning store.

"So they were trying to hire this guy for something," Haley said.

"It would appear so. I've been able to pull up a few additional emails between the two, including one that would indicate they finally came to an agreement."

Jones pulled up the extra emails on the screen so Recker and Haley could read them for themselves. It appeared that the two parties settled on a two-million-dollar payment. As they were reading, Jones continued working to find additional material.

"You were able to get all these just from an email address?" Haley asked.

"Well, it's a little more complicated than that. Email address, IP address, it all leads to something more substantial. I wasn't able to get into Jeremiah's computer system because they don't appear to be online at the moment. Our guy from Atlanta, Lee Tazlo, his computer was on. I was able to backdoor my way in and get the emails between the two parties."

"That's it," Recker said, getting an idea like a light bulb going off over his head.

"What?" Jones said.

"Can you definitely tell that Tazlo was hired to kill Vincent?"

"Not as of yet."

"Well, can you track him to see where he is?"

"I should be able to. Might take a day or two to track the bread crumbs. Why? What do you have in mind?"

"That we set a trap for him. Assuming he's here for Vincent."

"And what are you proposing?"

"If we do this right, we can get him before he makes another attempt."

"You still haven't said your plan," Jones replied.

"Well, can you send him an email, making it seem like it's coming from Jeremiah's computers?"

"Saying what?"

"Giving him bad information. Tell him you found out that Vincent's gonna be in a specific location on a certain day. If he replies in the affirmative, we know who's behind this. If he replies saying he doesn't know what you're talking about, then we got the wrong guy," Recker said.

"And what if he hears about what happened at the dry-cleaning store?"

"If you can send him something soon, he might respond by the time he hears something."

"Even if he does hear about it, he might not know it's Jeremiah's crew," Haley said. "He might not know where they're operating out of."

"That's true," Recker said. "If he's a hired gun, he probably doesn't know too much about their operation or where they're located. All he needs is the money and information on Vincent."

"What's the worst that could happen?" Haley asked.

"The worst is that he is indeed the guy we are looking for and he gets scared off thinking that we're on to him," Jones said. "Then he goes deeper into hiding and we have a tougher time locating him."

"It's worth the gamble," Recker said.

"And just how would we approach him?"

"I got something," Recker said, bumping Jones' chair over. "You set it up and I'll write down what to say."

Recker grabbed a pen and started writing down what he wanted Jones to say in the email. He wrote, "I heard from one of my sources that Vincent was shot. I haven't been able to confirm he's dead or not yet. What's the story?"

Jones read his note, not sure if it would work. "You think this will get it done?"

"One way to find out."

"Very well. I'll send the email, disguising it as coming from Jeremiah's crew."

"How complicated is that?" Haley asked.

"Child's play. Should only take me a few minutes."

"And then it's done?"

"Then it's done. And we pray that it works."

Jones sent the email only a few minutes later. They weren't going to just sit there and wait for a response, though. They couldn't be sure when one was coming, or if they'd be receiving one at all. Jones started retracing Tazlo's steps, trying to track his location from Atlanta to Philadelphia, if this was indeed where he was. As he dug into it deeper, he learned a little more about their suspected target. It appeared that he was working with someone.

"It seems that Mr. Tazlo has a partner," Jones said.

"How do you know?" Recker asked.

"From what I can gather, they bought two train tickets from Atlanta to Philadelphia about four weeks ago."

"Where'd they go from there?"

"Looks like a hotel. They checked out two weeks ago. I haven't been able to pinpoint exactly where they went from there."

"Timeline's matching up," Haley said. "They arrived four weeks ago. Then Vincent starts dodging bullets."

"Yeah. That's not a coincidence," Recker said.

They were hopeful that they'd get an email back from Tazlo, but it never came. They spent the rest of the night trying to determine his current location, though they couldn't. They called it a night and agreed to start up fresh again in the morning. Both Recker and Haley arrived back at the office early the next morning, about eight o'clock. Judging by the papers thrown about the desk, and the fact that Jones seemed like he was heavily into something, they surmised that he'd already been at it for a while.

"Did you even go to sleep?" Recker asked, knowing how his friend operated.

"Of course," Jones replied.

"Well, judging by how this place looks, you started a little before we did."

"Had a hard time sleeping. Got up early."

"How much early?"

"About two."

"What time'd you go to bed?"

"Midnight or so," Jones said, unconcerned.

"Hope it's been productive for you."

Jones got an uncomfortable smile on his face, probably due to the lack of sleep, and enthusiastically turned toward his partners as he delivered the news he was sure they'd like and appreciate.

"I've got them."

"Who?" Recker asked.

Jones' shoulders slumped, and the smile wiped away from his face. "What do you mean, who? The king and queen of England, who. Tazlo and his partner. I've got them."

"You're kidding."

"When was the last time I kidded about something like this?"

Recker tilted his head as he thought, looking up at the ceiling. "Never."

"Exactly."

"How?"

"Your plan worked. Our Mr. Tazlo responded to our email about five this morning," Jones said.

"What'd he say?"

"Here, read for yourself."

Jones pushed his chair away from the computer to let Recker and Haley have some room to look at the screen. Recker read the email aloud.

"Whoever told you that is blowing smoke up your ass. I'll let you know when he's dead."

"I guess that cinches it, doesn't it?" Recker said. "No doubt about it, he's our boy."

"So where's he at right now? We can surprise him and take him out," Haley said.

"He's staying at a small motel," Jones said. "But I don't think that would be our best move."

"Why not?" Recker asked.

"There's no doubt that he's got a partner for a reason."

"They're not staying together, are they?"

"No, they're not."

"Smart. If something goes wrong, something happens to one of them, the other completes the assignment."

"I think it will be better, easier, more convenient to take them both out at the same time," Jones said. "When they're making the hit."

"Yeah, but we don't know when that's gonna be."

Jones got another smile on his face. "We do now."

"When?"

"Noon today."

"Noon? That doesn't give us much time," Recker said.

"How'd you figure out the place?" Haley asked.

"After he replied to my initial email, I replied to his. I told him that we got an inside tip that Vincent was having a high-level emergency meeting at a place that would be perfect for a hit."

"You sly dog, you," Recker said, a grin on his face. "You set him up."

"Well, hopefully it will work."

"Where'd you tell him?"

"I made it for a restaurant in the northeast. Vincent's original home territory. There's a building directly across the street that's under construction. I told Tazlo that it would be a perfect spot to catch Vincent with a sniper rifle."

"We just need to get Vincent on board."

"Why? If we wait across the street, we can catch Tazlo and his partner as they start setting up."

"But what if they don't make themselves visible until Vincent arrives?" Jones asked.

"I'll call him and let him decide."

As Recker called Vincent, Jones and Haley started to go over plans, as well as pulling up pictures of the area. Jones was a little surprised that Recker joined them only a minute later.

"Did you call him?" Jones asked, looking for Recker's phone.

"Yep."

"That was a very short conversation."

"Wasn't much to talk about. I told him what the plan was, and he was in."

"Just like that?"

"Just like that. He wants to get this over with. He trusts us completely and is putting faith in us that we'll get the job done."

Recker leaned in and saw a few photos of the area and wanted to get down there as early as possible to go over where they could set up. The pictures were a good start, but there was only so much they could learn from the computer. They'd wind up getting there a couple of hours before the supposed assassination attempt, but Recker didn't mind waiting for a while if it meant finding their guy and eliminating him. Recker and Haley went over to the gun cabinet and grabbed some guns and ammo since they never reloaded after the dry-cleaning store battle. They left the office, threw their weapons in the back of Recker's SUV, and off they went.

"Hopefully Tazlo isn't setting up shop before we are," Haley said.

"The other issue is we still don't know what his partner looks like," Recker said.

They got to the restaurant in under half an hour and parked in the lot. They saw the building in construction across the street and walked over to it. It appeared to be a three-story office building, but the outsides weren't quite done yet as the windows hadn't been put in yet. They went around to the back of the building and slipped in through one of the windows. Recker motioned for Haley to check upstairs as he searched through the ground floor. After a few minutes, both reported the place was empty.

"Guess they don't work on the weekends," Haley said.

"I'll take the upstairs," Recker said, formulating the

plan in his mind. "Why don't you go across the street and keep an eye on here and let me know when someone's coming."

"What about us both staying here?"

"Both of us looking out a window is dicey. They could spot us and scare them away. I'll stay tucked down out of sight. That way you can alert me when they're coming, and we can get the jump on them."

Recker stayed on the second floor, sitting underneath one of the open windows as Haley jogged back across the street, clinging to a building next to the restaurant.

"You think they'll come early and try to get him on the way in?" Haley asked. "Or will they come later and get him on the way out?"

"I would think the sooner the better. That way they'll get two cracks at it. If they couldn't line up a shot when he first arrives, they can get him on the way out."

They waited until 11:30, when Haley saw a couple of characters walk across the street toward the empty building. They each had a black duffel bag in hand.

"Mike, got two headed your way with black bags. These gotta be the guys."

"All right. Let me know when they enter the building and hightail it over here."

"You got it," Haley said, waiting a minute until the two guys reached the building. "They're walking around to the back of the building now. I'm on the move."

"Got it."

Recker stood up, and though he had an assault rifle on his shoulder, removed his Glock from its holster. He always preferred using the hand gun whenever possible.

And with only two opponents, he figured that would do just fine. He thought about going down the steps to meet them, but quickly decided against it. If they were like him, they'd want to make sure the building was empty. Which meant they'd have to come to him. He could surprise them as they came up the steps. The only bad part was there was really no place to take cover since the building was still under construction. Recker thought he detected footsteps on the stairs, coming in his direction. He dropped to one knee to steady himself and raised his gun, aiming for the top of the stairs. A few seconds later, he saw the outline of a thinly built man reach the top of the stairs. Just as the man turned in Recker's direction, the Silencer surprised him by his presence and opened fire.

Recker dropped the man immediately, hitting him three times square in the chest. The man fell back, hitting the floor, the momentum of the fall causing him to fall back down the steps, rolling down until a loud thud was heard on the first floor. As soon as Recker heard the man's body hit the first floor, he heard more gunfire erupt. It sounded like Haley's gun. Recker started going down the stairs, then stopped about halfway as the gunfire stopped.

"Chris?"

"I'm here. We're all clear," Haley said.

Recker rushed down the steps and quickly located Haley, standing in the middle the room. He was standing over top of the body of Tazlo.

"Looks like our work here is done," Recker said.

"Yeah. I noticed your guy had a... little bit of a fall," Haley said with a smile a mile wide.

"All right, no sense in wasting any more time here. Let's get out of here."

"Gonna stick around for Vincent?"

"Yeah. Might as well tell him in person that it's over. Do me a favor and pull the car out of the lot and down the street. No sense in letting him know about you before it's necessary."

"Will do."

The two of them went back across the street to the restaurant. Haley pulled the car out as Recker waited by the front door. As he stood there waiting, the clouds became darker and rain started drizzling down. A short time later, Vincent's car pulled into the parking lot, right at twelve o'clock. Malloy was the first to get out of the back seat, who came around the bumper of the car to open the door for his boss. Before he pulled on the handle, he looked at Recker, who simply nodded, indicating that the coast was clear. Malloy took a quick look around, then finally opened the door, with Vincent stepping out of the car. Vincent also glanced around, looking a little uneasy. Recker quickly put his mind at ease.

"It's done with," Recker said. "It's over. You don't have anything to worry about anymore."

A relieved look overcame Vincent's face. He reached out his hand to shake Recker's, appreciative of his efforts. As they shook hands, the rain started beating down harder as the sounds of thunder played in the background above them.

"If you're interested and wanna see for yourself, they're lying in that building across the street that's under construction," Recker said, looking over at it.

Though he trusted that Recker was being truthful, he still sent one of his guys over to check it out. A couple of minutes later, the man returned, indicating that he saw the two bodies lying on the floor.

"Who were they?" Vincent asked.

"Outside guns," Recker said matter-of-factly. "The remnants of Jeremiah's crew hired them to take you out in retaliation for you taking out their boss. They knew you were behind it."

"So is that it?"

Recker threw his hand up, not completely sure of his answer. "Well, we haven't come up with anything else. So, I don't know if you can be too comfortable. But, these are the ones that tried the previous two times."

Though Vincent was happy with the developments, he still seemed slightly displeased. "Well, we both know there are still more of Jeremiah's men out there. May not be the last we've seen of them."

"If it makes you feel any better, I raided one of their spots the other day and found a payroll sheet with twenty names on it. I then took out six of them. Assuming there's not more somewhere, their numbers are dwindling. But that doesn't mean they couldn't make life rough for you. But they may have other things on their plate, like reorganizing, or just surviving."

Vincent nodded, seeming a little more upbeat. "I can't thank you enough for the swiftness in your actions in concluding this matter."

"Well, I did owe you," Recker said. "I would say this squares us though."

"Indeed it does."

"I'll be seeing you."

Recker turned away from the group and walked past the restaurant, going down the street until he got to the car, where Haley was waiting for him. Vincent and Malloy watched him for a minute, before talking about their next course of business.

"What now, boss?" Malloy asked.

"Well, since we're already here at this fine establishment, we might as well have a celebratory luncheon."

"And after that?"

"One thing at a time, Jimmy. It's a beautiful day today, is it not?" Vincent asked, looking up at the sky and letting the rain splash down onto his face.

Malloy looked up and shrugged. "I guess so, sir."

"Remember when we first met Recker, I told you we'd give him a long leash, that one day he would prove useful to us."

"I was always doubtful. You turned out to be right, though."

"Yes. Our friend, Mr. Recker, has become a powerful ally for us," Vincent said, looking up at the rain again. "No doubt about it. It sure is a beautiful day."

ABOUT THE AUTHOR

Mike Ryan lives in Pennsylvania, with his wife, and four kids. He is the bestselling author of The Silencer Series, The Cain Series, The Eliminator Series, as well as numerous other books. Visit his website at www.mikeryanbooks.com to find out more about his books, and sign up for his newsletter.

facebook.com/mikeryanauthor

instagram.com/mikeryanauthor

ALSO BY MIKE RYAN

The Cain Series

The Ghost Series

The Eliminator Series

The Extractor Series

The Brandon Hall Series

The Last Job

A Dangerous Man

The Crew

Made in the USA
Middletown, DE
11 September 2021